MW01408447

Dedicated to Aidan, Charlotte, Nadja, and Tyler
Also to our friend Brandon, the strongest guy we know

INC

is brought to you by

Neil Blevins	Jeremy Cook	Jeremy Vickery	Gio Nakpil
Bill Zahn	Chris Stoski	Dominic Qwek	Mohammad Modarres
Stephan Bugaj	Christina Davis	Heidi Taillefer	Nathan Fariss

Journal editor : Brenda Zahn
Cover artwork : Neil Blevins
Back cover artwork : Neil Blevins & Bill Zahn
Legal help : Lynn Bartsch, Seth Steinberg

A
soulburn studios
production

The Story Of INC
Copyright © 2017 Soulburn Press
All rights reserved.

All text and artwork in this book are copyright © 2017 Neil Blevins, Bill Zahn, and Stephan Bugaj unless otherwise noted.

No part of this book may be reproduced or transmitted in any form or by any means electronic or mechanical, including photocopying, xerography, and video recording, without the written permission from the publisher

The following groups provided stock photos for use in this project:
Dreamstime, HDRI Flares, hdrmaps, Jason Bickerstaff, Rus S/Shutterstock.com, Jag_cz/Shutterstock.com, NASA_JPL, Jewish photography nucleus, PHOTOBASH.org

All other photographs, textures, models, etc were created by the Inc artists.

Development: Teena Apeles, Sara Richmond, Xiao Qing Chen

Final Layout: Paul J. Salamoff
Printing by Mark Vierra at onthemark.net

www.soulburnstudios.com
info@soulburnstudios.com
Printed In China

Standard Edition
ISBN: 978-0-9992032-0-0
Library of Congress Control Number: 2017911117

First Edition, November 2017
10 9 8 7 6 5 4 3 2 1

TABLE OF CONTENTS

The Historian			06
The Book of Landis			17
Chapter 01	▲	A Cruel Creator	19
Chapter 02	▲	No Safety in Numbers	31
Chapter 03	▲	A Perilous Awakening	53
Chapter 04	▲	Of Friends & Enemies	93
Chapter 05	▲	A Collision of Consciences	105
The World of INC			119
The Making of INC			159

is the story of my best friend INC,
e his life so that you might have yours.

THE HISTORIAN 7

Those are the first words of The Book of Landis, a book from a past long forgotten by most of us.

A time when our planet was a desert planet. When the ocean basins and river gullies were bone dry, and not a drop of rain fell from the sky. Now we call this "the time before the waters". Then it was simply known as how things had always been.

I am our people's historian, and it is my task to keep alive the story of how our present day society came to be.

Very little is known about our past, for the waters themselves erased the books and buildings of the old world, and the changes wrought by the waves washed away the old ways. Few who lived in that time of change felt the need to recall their bitter past.

From the story written in his own words, and the few images preserved from that time, we have recreated this historical record to the best of our ability.

Much of that time has been lost, but I hope to give you a sense of what it was like in this forgotten age. A sense of what it was like for my humble ancestor Landis, his humbler-still robot, and their quest borne of love which ended in the greatest change our world has ever known.

THE HISTORIAN

Before we delve into the Book Of Landis, a bit about our world.

A thousand years before Landis was born and INC was built, The First Descendants of The Fallen Fathers wandered our world. They found ancient plants dried into fossils by the hot sun, chipped away by dusty winds, which hinted at water that was nowhere to be found except in small amounts deep ¬below the sands. But the deep wells could only provide so much water, and soon The First Descendants began to die.

THE HISTORIAN

As their numbers grew thin, The First Descendants stumbled upon the towering structure that came to be known as *The Citadel*. Looming over the distant horizon the massive, metal and strange building was a terrifying sight at first. Frightened, the caravan stayed back.

The council of The First Descendants convened to debate the origin and purpose of this monolith. Was it sent to save them or destroy them? And sent by whom? A friend? An enemy? The Gods?

THE STORY OF INC

THE HISTORIAN

Nobody understood the nature of The Citadel and all were afraid to find out for fear of another cataclysm one generation after the disaster which had caused the fall of The Fallen Fathers -- the event which destroyed our race's old world and stranded us on this one.

But in time desperation overcame fear. The First Descendants approached the citadel with trepidation, but their fear was soon replaced by jubilation. The secret of The Citadel was there to save them.

They built their the city around The Citadel and the leaders of The First Descendants formed the priesthood that watched over it, daily giving thanks to The Gods for their salvation, and protecting this temple of life from infidels and usurpers.

Before long some people were forced out of the Oasis, and others left of their own accord, for long forgotten reasons. The descendants of these outcasts became The Wanderers, people who moved from deep well to deep well, staying barely alive off what little water and food could be found in The Wastelands.

Landis was born a Wanderer. He might have stayed one forever, too, if it wasn't for his wife's untimely death and the desperate struggle to preserve his unborn child that led to the creation of INC -- the robot whose friendship with a human changed our world forever.

And now I present to you, The Book of Landis.

THE STORY OF INC

THE HISTORIAN

THE STORY OF INC

THE BOOK *of* LANDIS

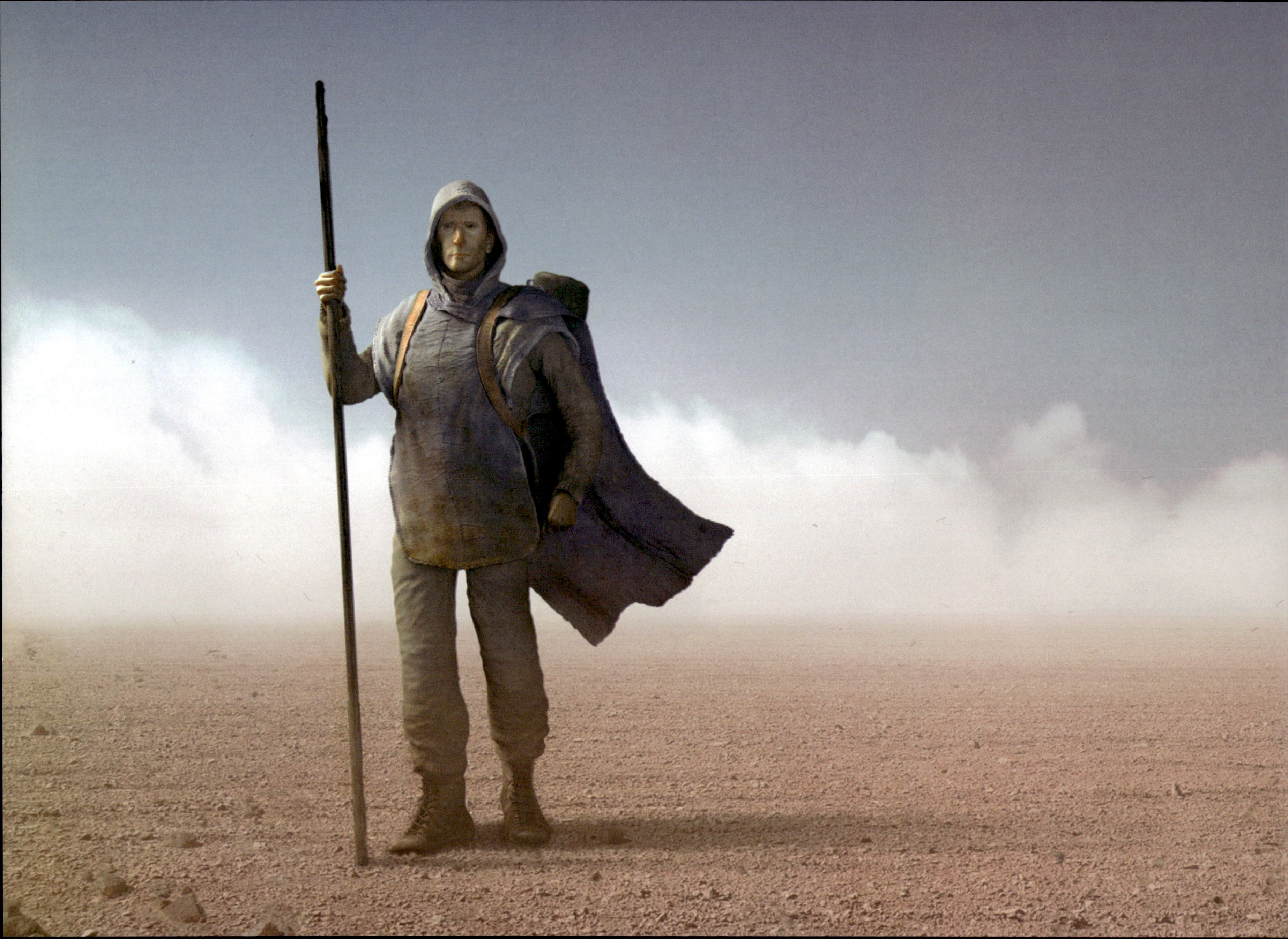

Chapter 01
A CRUEL CREATOR

Thankfully, my only daughter, you will never know what a world of desolation can do to someone's soul. I will be forever grateful that I got to see you grow, and become the hard-working woman you are today.

Please always remember, every time you drink a sip of clean water, that it was not always this way. Many nomads roamed the Coral Barrens, tortured by what at one time, a millennium ago, was a vast sea.

Only rumors and legends remain of what happened, what disaster struck this small planet and left us a stranded people willing to wander miles for a desperate sip from a muddy puddle.

Generation after generation suffered, but the strong found a way to persist and survive.

Once an oasis was found, word spread quickly.

So to say I was less then optimistic about our prospects would be an understatement. To be honest, the Coral Barrens had become home. A cruel, heartless, desolate home where you would never stay in the same place more than a day. You followed the water, or fled the beasts that would make you their next meal.

Nevertheless, your mother was always the optimist, and her sights were set on having a family - in the Oasis.

"You're a fool if you think this is it," she would say, "that there isn't something about to happen. That the Creators don't have something big in mind for you."

Unfortunately, the Creators did have something in mind for her, and I hated them for those plans, because those plans took her away from you and me.

"Promise me that you will find a way," she said, her voice soft and barely a whisper. "Promise me you won't give up, and that you will bring what's left of our family to the Oasis. You need to find that part of you that believes."

I didn't believe, but for her sake, I told her I did.

"I promise," I said, "with everything I have."

With that, she left this world, and me alone for what I thought would be the rest of my short days.

I loved your mother, and all I had was my word. That's when an old-world bot named INC entered our lives.

Bots at one time had been the backbone of the old world, serving mostly as construction and repairing mech. Now only a few remained, and they were in bad shape. Parts were hard to come by, and in the end, humans were cheaper.

I once overheard a merchant say, "Humans can heal, bots can't."

Most of my livelihood relied on the fact that bots were seen as more work than they were worth. I could fix almost anything, and with few spare parts to be found, I had built a reputation as someone who could find clever solutions.

That was also the problem with bots - their simple nature. They knew how to work by the book, but thinking outside the box, or looking for an inventive solution to a no-win situation, was out of their scope.

I was clever, bots were dumb, and if any merchant employed a bot over me, I considered them an idiot.

Now I found myself in need of one, and hated the idea of interacting with a glorified toaster.

"That one might work better," I said, pointing to a bot that was powered down and resting in the corner of a peddler's tent. The rusty and worn bot seemed to be held together with nothing more than luck.

The merchant wasn't having it.

"No, this one," he said. "Good model."

He again motioned toward a squat, little bot standing next to him that had one flickering, malfunctioning eye and looked like it could burst into flames any minute.

"Tell me about the one in the corner," I said.

"The red one?" the peddler replied. "Junk."

Maybe he was right, I thought. I again looked at the small, wobbly bot at his side - its eye flickering at me. It now had a little puddle of "fluid" underneath it on the ground.

"You know what?" I said. "I'll take my chances with the red one."

I quickly but carefully made the crucial modifications. It wasn't much more complicated than most cooling systems on a mech, but this one needed to serve a much more important function.

With my fingers crossed and a hopeful prayer, I powered up the rusty bot.

"Core system computer initialized," said a monotone, digital voice. It continued, confirming system after system was activated. Then, a pause. I waited with bated breath.

"Additional systems … recognized … initiating … All systems at 100%."

I breathed a sigh of relief. Then, the lights in his eyes flickered on and power seemed to activate his limbs, and he stood upright.

"Hello, what task would you have me perform?" he asked, looking directly at me and speaking in a much more … "human" tone.

Most bots existed to serve various merchants, working endlessly until they literally fell apart. INC was a welder bot, and his looks and demeanor told me he wasn't far from suffering the fate of most bots.

Now, his days of working for merchants were over.

"Make sure all your internal systems remain functioning at 100%," I said.

"So, I don't have to weld anymore?" he asked.

"No," I replied. "You work for me now. So … you know."

THE BOOK OF LANDIS

INC was my first and only bot, and I was used to competing with them for employment, so to say our first exchange was awkward would be an understatement.

"Actually," he replied, "I'm sorry, I don't know."

"Just … do what I say and follow me," I said, "okay?"

"How should I address you?" he asked. "Customary salutations are mister, sir, boss …"

"Landis," I replied. "Now, can we please just focus on the journey ahead?"

From that moment on, INC followed me like a diligent puppy.

Our first week or so together was spent mainly in silence. He would often, to my frustration, watch me perform the most menial of tasks, then try to mimic the way I did things in some attempt to be more human, or maybe to fit in, I'm not sure.

Most bots were quirky. They were hundreds of years old, had been through multiple owners and were always reminded of their place in relation to people. They were expected to work, and nothing else.

So I just wasn't used to having any kind of actual conversation with one, let alone one that asked things like: "The sky is a very nice shade of blue … why?"

THE BOOK OF LANDIS 23

THE STORY OF INC

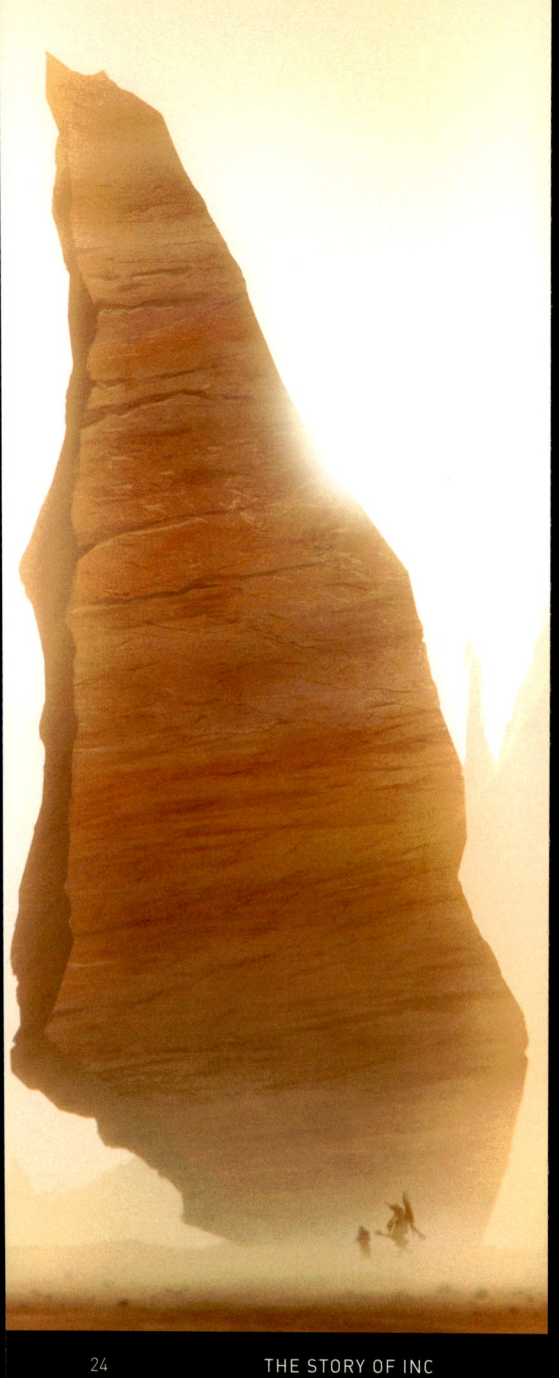

I just shrugged my shoulders.

I guess because of his fairly recent change in occupation, INC finally had time to contemplate the world in which he lived. Everything for INC was a new, wonderful mystery.

"This planet has a lot of dirt," he said. "Why?"

"I don't know. How are your systems?"

"100%," he replied.

"Good," I said. "Why don't you start a campfire before it gets dark?"

I'll give him this, INC picked things up quickly, creating makeshift shelters while I slept, or keeping watch while I gathered what water I could find.

For some reason, he seemed grateful, in his own weird way, for the fact that he was now in my service. As if I had saved him from something.

I never let on that once he had served his purpose, I would be selling him to fund my new life in the Oasis.

As I slept, I heard INC's cold, digital computer voice say, "Cooling system at 92%. Water required."

"Sorry," INC said. "We should get water soon."

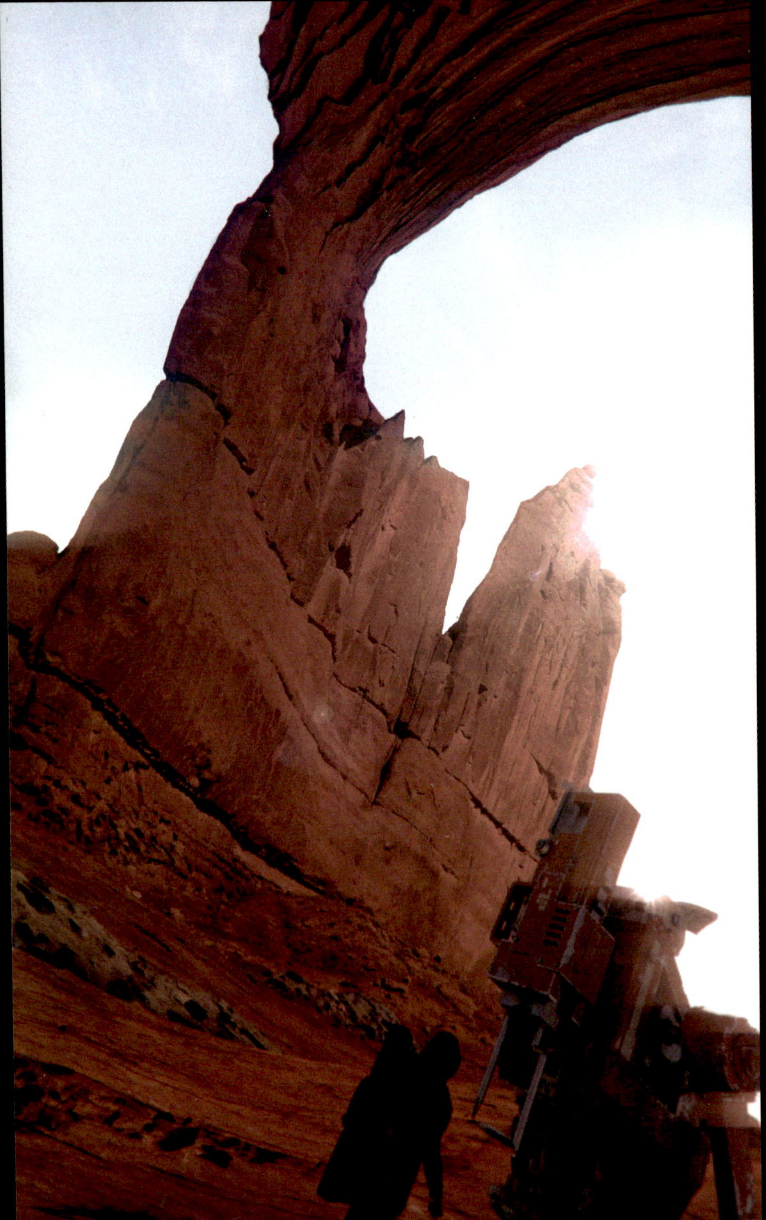

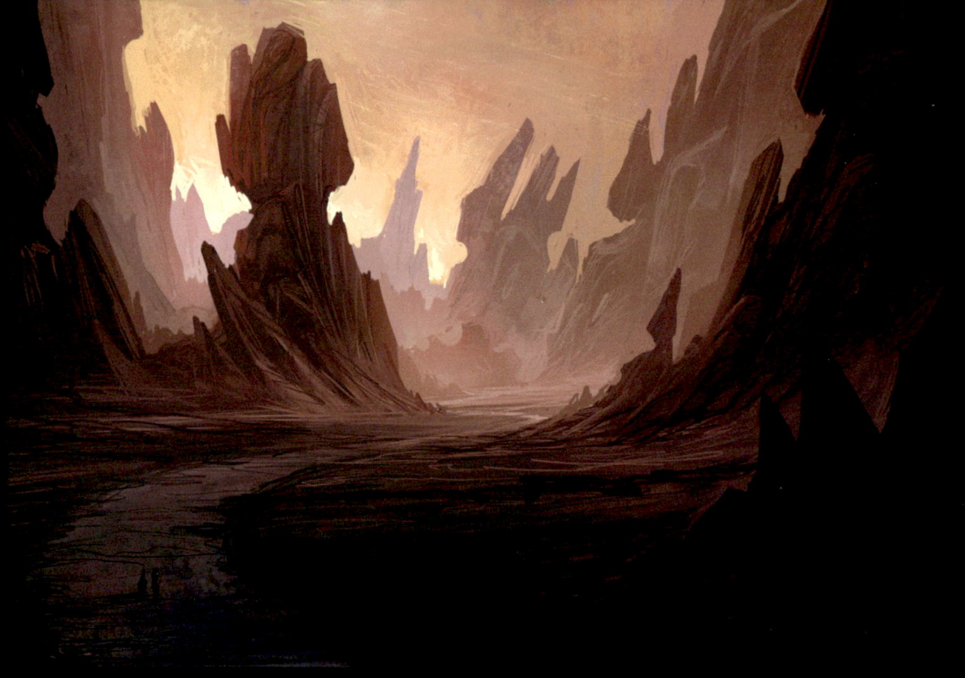

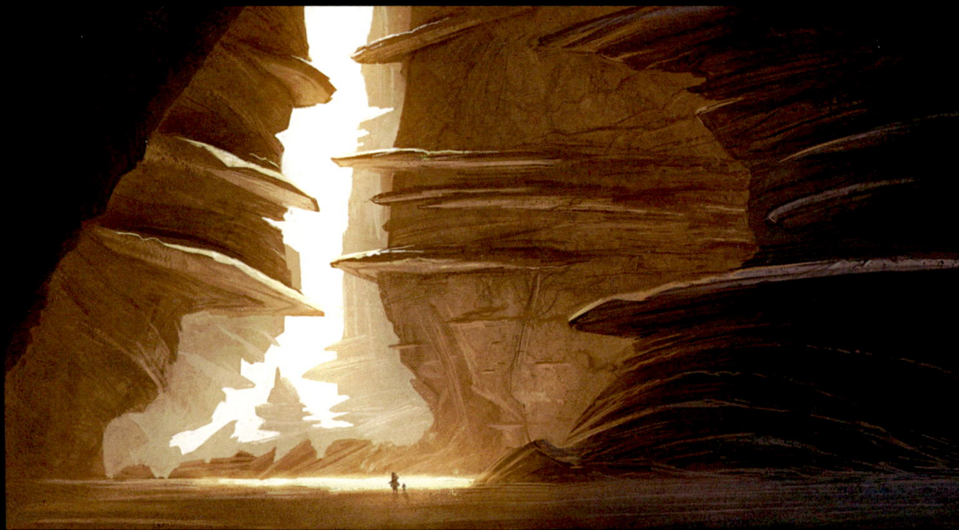

Now when you had to travel like we did, you followed the water, and when you couldn't find a natural source, which was most of the time, you had to find a peddler's caravan.

"How do you find them?" INC asked.

"Either follow their deep tracks in the dirt," I replied, "or look for their large flags and banners."

These guys were the worst of the worst. They smuggled "repurposed" water from the Oasis, generally filtered waste or runoff that was sold at a steep profit. They often toyed with the weaker migrants, and abused the power they held.

"Don't say a word," I told INC. "I want to avoid trouble."

With my eyes down, I quickly approached the camp, trying to avoid eye contact with anyone. At the nearest merchant, I threw my money on the table and grabbed two jugs.

"Nice try."

Almost immediately, I felt one of the jugs being yanked from my hand.

"Water is a privilege, not a right," the merchant said. "Your rusty companion can fend for himself."

THE STORY OF INC

I threw more money on his table.

"What I use the water for is none of your business," I said as his wife glared at me from the corner of the tent, and I added, "… at least my companion smells better."

With that, he swiped the other jug out of my hand.

Now in hindsight, I will admit I was quick to temper, and after all that had happened, I wasn't in the best state of mind.

Without warning, I tackled the merchant to the ground and was ready to pummel him into unconsciousness. I can't explain what came over me - the anger, the surge of emotions.

"My life won't be determined by a condescending lunatic," I yelled at him.

My fist was about to land squarely on his nose when I saw INC watching me. All I can say is something in that dumb bot's eyes made me stop my attack. If it weren't for him, I may have killed that slimy merchant.

Before I could release him, his wife offered to sell me a secret to spare his life. I played it up as if I felt conflicted, visibly tightening my fist.

I glared into the man's eyes. "You're lucky your wife is the smart one."

I finally agreed to take her offer … and both jugs of water.

"Why are we walking so fast?" INC asked as we hurried away.

"I had to do what I had to do back there, okay?" I said.

"Of course," he said. "Why are we in such a hurry?"

"There's going to be a funeral ceremony just outside the Oasis in two days," I replied.

"A funeral means a death, and a death means an open spot. Our luck might have changed."

It was now a race. Not only did we have to get to the Oasis, but we had to get there first.

Although I knew better, I pushed us day and night, sometimes taking shortcuts we should have avoided. We were nearly devoured several times.

Of course, INC just watched in wonder as one critter or another would try to chew and tug on his metal limbs in an attempt to steal them away.

Initially, I couldn't decide if he was just amazingly curious, or if he had more than a few circuits loose. Not to mention the constant questions. Day and night, questions. Sitting by the campfire, questions. Climbing a ravine, questions.

"Where did all the water go?" "Why are your eyes blue?" "Why do males have nipples?"

Most of the time, I just kept moving as if I didn't hear him. I did have to admit, the more he seemed to observe and get a chance to interact with everything, the more and more complex his questions became.

"That's strange," INC said. "Do you think that's a natural formation or …"

"If you ask me one more …" I stopped when I saw what he was looking at.

THE STORY OF INC

Chapter 02
NO SAFETY IN NUMBERS

Among the irregular landscape of the desert, a perfect rectangle reached up into the heavens.

It was bigger and more majestic than I had ever imagined, dominating everything it surrounded with a strange benevolence.

"No," I said. "That's going to be our new home."

"Why does …"

"Shhh," I said. "Can I just enjoy the moment, please?"

We cautiously made our way closer to the city built in the shadow of the Citadel. What at first appeared insignificant now seemed impenetrable. Tall walls circled the place, and guard towers served as a reminder that you were watched at all times.

"Are they trying to keep people out, or in?" INC asked.

"Definitely out," I replied. "We just need to wait for the funeral."

As we made camp just out of sight, my stomach ached with both excitement and nervous energy as I stared at the spectacle of lights - the way they shimmered and bounced off the immense tower they surrounded.

The one thing that stuck out the most, something my eyes had never seen before, was an odd dancing of the light off one of the tower's walls. It created such a strange, yet beautiful, pattern.

I smiled as I realized it was the light bouncing and reflecting off water onto the walls of the Citadel. But the happy feeling was tinged with pain. I was gazing at the sight your mother only dreamt of seeing. Now I just had to get in, and keep my promise.

I slept that night with nothing but dreams of water - what it would be like to be completely submerged in water, to be surrounded by it.

With an annoying finger-poking to my side, INC woke me up just as the sun was rising.

"Dammit INC," I protested, "I'm sleeping."

"Is that what you call a funeral?" he asked.

The Oasis' large gates had opened, and a procession was emerging. Led by men in large, ornate cloaks, a group carried a shrouded body on planks of dried wood.

"If not, that guy's gonna be shocked when he wakes up," I said with a stupid smile on my face.

INC just looked confused.

"I can see you're gonna be a barrel of laughs," I said. "Yes, that's a funeral."

We watched as they draped flowers and mementos onto the body.

"Was this person important?" INC asked.

I shrugged my shoulders. "Probably not. For humans, death is a big deal. It's a sign of respect, I guess … honor their memory."

With great reverence, clerics held torches to the dried wood, lighting a funeral pyre that quickly consumed the body.

INC watched the mourners intently, with their wailing and tears of grief.

"It seems we may not be the only ones to have heard the news," I said.

I pointed to a dust cloud off to our right. Migrants, heading for the gates.

THE BOOK OF LANDIS

I sprinted with everything I had. INC, on the other hand, was definitely not built for speed, and looked more like a bumbling toddler in his awkward gait.

Now when you're in the moment, full of desperation and dying of thirst, you may not realize how others perceive you. The poor mourners and priests must have thought they were under attack as they saw both us and the other migrants racing toward them.

"Sound the alarms!" cried one of the guards.

The mourners quickly rushed for the safety of the Oasis. Guards in the towers were ready and drew rifles. This clearly wasn't the first time they had been ambushed by migrants.

They slammed the gates shut on us.

"Dammit!" I yelled.

"Dammit!" INC mimicked, then looked at me for some kind of approval - which I didn't give.

Suddenly, gunshots rang out. At the time, I didn't realize they were warning shots.

I frantically searched INC for damage.

"All systems are still at 100%," INC assured.

By the time I felt confident that he was fine, the other migrants, a small family with two children and some elderly, were already speaking with a cleric.

"That's it," I said. "It's over."

Without warning, the guards began shoving the family away from the gates, pointing their weapons at the frightened group.

"Hey, take it easy," I yelled, but then I found the guards aiming their rifles at me.

In a desperate move, the mother tried lifting her children over the wall, begging for anyone to take them. She and her crying offspring were shoved away.

The Oasis had its policies, one of which was no orphans.

"That one," said a voice from the tower.

Suddenly, two guards grabbed me by the arms and led me in past the devastated family. They watched with tears as INC and I were escorted through the huge gates.

To this day, I still don't know that family's fate, or what struggles they had to endure, but I will never forget their tortured faces as the gates were closed on them.

"You will remain quiet," the guard ordered. "Only speak when spoken to, and do not touch anything."

Before us towered the Citadel. I had to arch my neck as far as it would go to try and even see the top. It reached to the sky, and vanished into the clouds. The base glistened with droplets of water.

Floating at the corners were very large, ominous metallic heads, each easily the size of a man. The strange faces were still and fixed, but their gaze … I don't know how to describe it - their gaze was unmoving, but, alive.

As we passed them, a cleric informed us not to make eye contact with the "angels." I readily followed his instructions.

Within the walls, the Oasis was a bustling city with a busy market place, and even some farmland. This was better than I had even imagined.

What amazed me most were the people. No one was in a hurry, or scared. They just seemed to be living - buying and selling goods and going about their seemingly carefree lives.

We walked past people working in the market selling greens that were fresh and vibrant. Others sold their linens and handmade pottery. Everything was available to anyone who wanted it.

"Eyes forward, keep moving," the guard shouted, pushing me from behind.

I noticed the expressions on people's faces changed the moment they saw us. They were leery of the dirty outsiders.

Along with blacksmith shops and woodworkers, we passed a small recycling area filled with old mechanical parts, wood, metals and, unfortunately, non-functioning bots of all types just piled up with reckless abandon. Most old-world bots at this point had been run into the ground, and were now seen as relics of the past.

INC stopped in his tracks, his eyes locked on the discarded shells of rusted, forgotten bots. Then, he looked at me as if he had something to say. I shook my head - now was not the time.

I'm not sure if he was simply hoping he might find parts in the pile, or was he suddenly faced with the realization of his own mortality? I now regret that it was probably the latter.

We were then led past curious but distrusting citizens into a secluded building.

"Hold still," a technician ordered. "Have you ever had strange bleeding from the eyes or ears, wounds that refuse to heal or strange discoloration of the skin?"

I shook my head.

They handled us with the assumption that we were disease ridden. No one seemed interested in actually talking to us. They didn't want to know us.

My guess is, if I didn't pass the physical exam, we would be booted out immediately, and it's hard to kick someone out once you know their name.

There are plenty of diseases, parasites and other ailments the badlands can inflict on a person, and the Oasis was not about to let someone infect their healthy populace. I was terrified for multiple reasons about what they might find.

Suddenly, everything stopped and a well-dressed cleric entered. He was an older, distinguished man, and by his clothes, probably the highest ranking in the settlement.

He looked at INC with a bit of trepidation, and introduced himself as Cleric Graton.

"Your bot, he … it carries some organic matter in its interior compartment," he said. "Explain."

That's where it got awkward. How could I explain what INC was carrying? How I took an ordinary welder bot and turned him into essentially, well …

"I'm pregnant!" INC said. He seemed quite proud, which was really annoying.

"No!" I quickly corrected. "No, he's carrying a cryogenically frozen embryo."

Graton watched us both with fascination, but it didn't last long. Another cleric quickly spoke up.

"I'm sorry," he said. "We have rules. One death inside the walls means one outsider gains admission. You and an embryo now constitute two people."

Before we could blink, guards were rushing us toward the gates.

"Gentlemen," Graton said, "wouldn't you agree, this should be debated by the council? It would make for a fascinating topic."

Initially, none of them seemed convinced, until one finally but reluctantly agreed. The others slowly fell into line.

"Thanks," I whispered.

Graton gave me a nod.

We were whisked away to a desolate corner far from the others as they decided our fate. All we could do was watch and wait. Even worse, while they debated, we were not allowed to partake of citizen liberties, such as food or water.

From a distance, we watched the elders debating amongst themselves, making a great show of their intellect to one another, trying to outdo the others with great feats of philosophical thought, with exaggerated hand gestures to match.

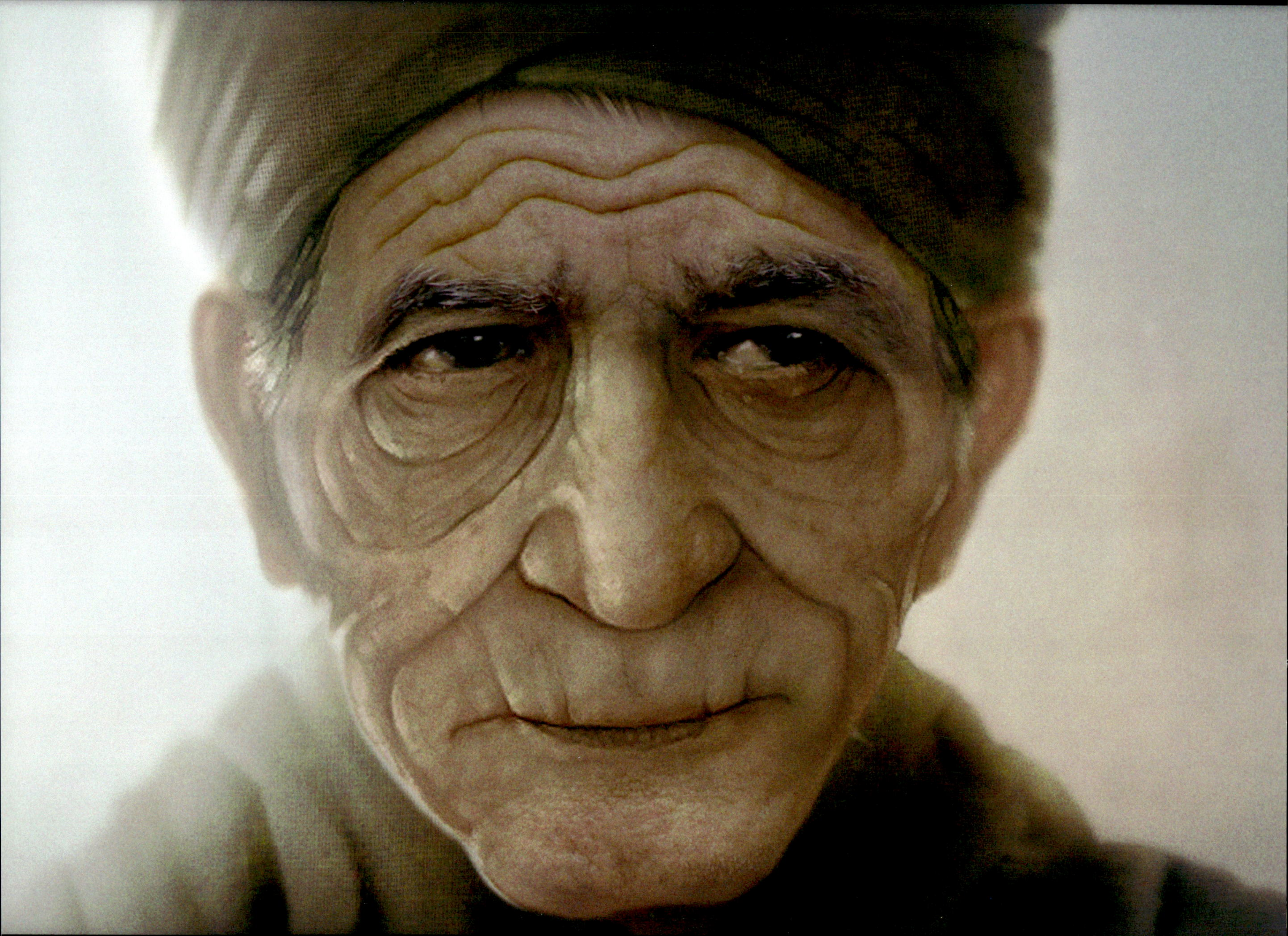

"What do you think they're saying?" INC asked.

"Kick the fool out," I replied.

A young woman approached them with a large pitcher.

They raised the cups they kept on long, ornate scarves tied around their necks. She slowly poured them each a full cup of water.

I watched as the clean, crystal-clear water flowed into their wooden cups.

But then my gaze quickly shifted to her. She had vibrant eyes, and her face was perfection. A face that had not seen the hardships and pain of life in the badlands.

"Is it acceptable to stare at females?" INC asked.

"What? No!" I replied, quickly trying to hide the fact that I was staring.

When I again discreetly glanced in her direction, the young woman was staring back at me.

It startled me at first, but I gave her a small smile. I was happy to see a small one returned.

"She seems to think it's acceptable …" INC started.

"Shut up, INC," I whispered through my smile.

Noticing my exchange with the woman, Graton quickly sent her away.

"The cleric doesn't seem to think it's acceptable …" INC said.

"I should have gone with the bot with the twitchy eye and bladder issues," I quipped.

As night fell, it was clear they were no closer to a decision, which meant our chances faded with every hour.

My thirst grew, and I knew it would be another painful night of head-pounding dehydration.

Although what little hope I had was vanishing, I asked INC, "How are your systems?"

"94%," INC replied.

He could sense my concern.

"That should hold until morning," he added. "Get some rest."

That night, I returned to my regular dreams: wandering in the dark, a mouthful of dust, watching my skin crack, crumble and blow away in the wind.

Just as the sun began to rise, I felt my side being poked by a metal finger again.

"Finger-poking's your thing, isn't it?" I asked.

"Sorry," he replied, "cooling systems at 87%."

While the embryo was kept frozen by liquid nitrogen, INC relied on water to maintain his own cooling system. If he failed, the embryo failed.

I tried to spot someone, anyone, who might give us a bit of water. I had some money to bribe them, anything for water. But no one had woken yet. The place was silent - so I made my move.

"Do you think this is the wisest …" INC began to ask.

I guess the annoyed look on my face gave him the answer.

I quietly and covertly made my way across the Oasis toward the huge monolithic structure. Water glistened off it and slowly trickled from small slits in the side. All I needed to gather was a few cups' worth.

I pulled from my pack a small, wooden cup. No one would even notice a cupful missing. If anything, the water seemed to be just trickling into a small mud puddle, completely wasted. At least I was going to put it to good use.

Making sure no eyes were on me, I slowly approached the wall.

"Stop!" a cleric ordered. Apparently not everyone had been asleep. For some reason, I ignored the order.

I was just about to put my cup to the wall when the ground shook under my feet, sending me backward onto the dirt. It was as if the building had come to life.

From the corner of the structure, one of the massive heads raised from where it had been floating and came alive. The ground exploded upward from around the huge metallic head, revealing it had a body below the soil. I looked right at it, and it fixed its gaze on me.

My gut told me this was not going to end well.

It immediately swiped its arms at me as I ran for the nearest structure I could find.

People quickly emerged from their dwellings, alarmed by the commotion, only to just as quickly run back inside to hide when they saw my panicked face rushing toward them.

"Take cover!" I yelled.

Except INC, with his odd trot, who came bolting over to defend me.

"I'll save you!"

"No!" I yelled. "I said take cover!"

Of course, he didn't listen. The guardian swung at me, sending me to the ground.

That's when I felt INC's arms grabbing me off the ground and dragging me back. I berated him for risking his safety.

I said things I wish I could take back.

When I finally caught my breath, a crowd had gathered. I had failed to notice that the robot had stopped dead in its tracks, and was now returning to its position.

As I lay there, angry faces stared us down. Several structures and homes had been damaged.

THE BOOK OF LANDIS

THE STORY OF INC

THE BOOK OF LANDIS

46   THE STORY OF INC

"He tried to take the water directly from the temple," a cleric cried from the tower. "He awoke one of the guardians."

Clearly, this was about more than just stealing water. This was the worst of sins.

The disgust on the citizens' faces was palpable. We had soiled, in their eyes, sacred ground.

Furious guards rushed INC and me toward the gates. I tried to make our case, pleading our ignorance. We respected the gods, and had learned our lesson.

"I'm sorry," INC said. "Next time I will shut down other systems first."

Nothing mattered now except the realization of the misery that awaited us outside those gates - the fate of INC, then finally, my only hope for a family and fulfilling my promise.

We were thrown out, and the large gates slowly closed. Before they could fully seal, a figure suddenly emerged, running toward us. It was the young woman. When she'd made it about halfway, she stopped and looked around in amazement, tinged with fear.

Gathering herself, she took a deep breath and walked in our direction.

THE BOOK OF LANDIS

"I've never been outside the gates before," she said, handing me two jugs of water.

Several clerics rushed to the gates, and ordered her to return with the water.

"I have to know your name," I said.

Before she could tell me, from the gates, Graton yelled, "Asha!"

"I'm taking a stand," she yelled. "I won't return until I am heard."

Graton slowly and cautiously emerged from the gates, trying to keep the tone calm.

It was clear this was his daughter. Otherwise, her fate would have been the same as ours.

"There are penalties for stealing water. He stole water. Now, you've stolen water. Not only that, you are giving it to outsiders." He said again, "There are penalties."

Although terrified by the prospect of life outside the gates, she refused to return to the safety of the Oasis.

"Come back with the water, make a penance, and maybe," he said, "maybe you will receive a light sentence."

I offered the vessels back to her, but she refused to take them.

"I'm sick of hearing babies whimper their last breaths outside our gates," she said. "I won't turn people away to die anymore. There are others who think like me."

Graton pleaded with her. "Asha, these are the rules of the Creators. They will take away the water if the rules aren't followed."

"I can see you won't listen," she said, "that none of you will change."

To her father's devastation, she finally turned away from him and walked past us toward the abyss that is the badlands.

For someone like her, it was certain death, but she was determined to make a point.

I don't know, maybe I felt something for her, or maybe it was the father/child thing, but I found myself doing something I would never do. I quickly grabbed her and began dragging her back toward the Oasis.

She fought and called me names even I hadn't heard before. She was pretty creative.

As soon as we reached the gates, guards took her from me. I could hear her demanding release as they disappeared into the walled city.

I handed the water jugs back to Graton.

"I'm sorry, but I didn't realize," I said. "Tell everyone inside I'm sorry. We were simply … thirsty."

His eyes were grateful, but his face stern. He returned one of the jugs to me. "Go, be safe, and may the Creators be with you in your travels."

He retreated into the city, and the gates closed on us.

I stood there and listened as they secured the gate, as the locks were set in place.

"I know I have a tendency to get on your nerves," INC said, "but our current water issue …"

I handed him the jug. That would give us about two days to find the next source.

We headed northwest. Generally that time of year, merchants could be found in the Coral Barrens.

I ordered INC to make camp before it got dark.

I looked back, and although we were now miles away, I could still see the tower, and the dim lights that illuminated it.

As we sat by the campfire, I was too caught up in myself and my stupidity to deal with INC. I had one promise to keep, and one life to save, and I had blown it.

INC just fiddled with his welding torch, cleaning and repairing it. I figured old programming died hard.

I can generally read humans, but a bot, well, they're not quite as easy. It didn't help that I was completely indifferent to anything he might be thinking.

Then, he turned to me and began asking questions. Not the usual ones about how this or that worked, but ones that were a bit more difficult. He asked of gods and men, of dogma and blasphemy. I struggled, giving trite answers to things I didn't even understand.

"The Creators are probably long dead," I said, "or they simply don't care anymore."

"Do the Creators know about bots?" he asked.

It was odd for a bot, but he genuinely seemed upset by what he saw as a lack of purpose for him in creation.

"I have no idea," I replied. "It's time to shut down for the night and stop wasting water."

That's when INC turned to me, and thanked me again.

"You have given me purpose in creation," he said. "While you are not the Creator, you are my creator, and soon, I will be the creator of new life. I will always remember what you have done for me. No other bot has ever been so fortunate.

Maybe," he continued, "I won't be a forgotten bot in a scrap pile."

With that, he seemed content and shut down for the night. I didn't have the heart to tell him that we were both doomed to be forgotten husks soon enough.

Before I fell asleep, I found myself just watching him with, for what was the first time, sympathy.

He looked at me one last time. Then, the digital voice coldly stated, "Initiating sleep mode. Systems at 99%."

THE BOOK OF LANDIS

THE STORY OF INC

Chapter 03
A PERILOUS AWAKENING

The sound that woke us up was indescribable. It was thunderous, followed by the eerie sound of metal twisting and breaking.

It echoed through the night, off the canyon walls, and carried for miles.

Looking in the direction of the Oasis, the Citadel was brighter than ever, lit by what appeared to be fire within the confines of the city. Large pillars of smoke rose to the sky.

We watched as there were occasional large flashes of light - what looked like explosions. Then, it all seemed to die down, smoke billowing from around the massive structure.

As the sun rose, the smoke slowly subsided and just left a haze over the Oasis - the Citadel emerging and towering above whatever devastation had happened below.

THE STORY OF INC

THE BOOK OF LANDIS 55

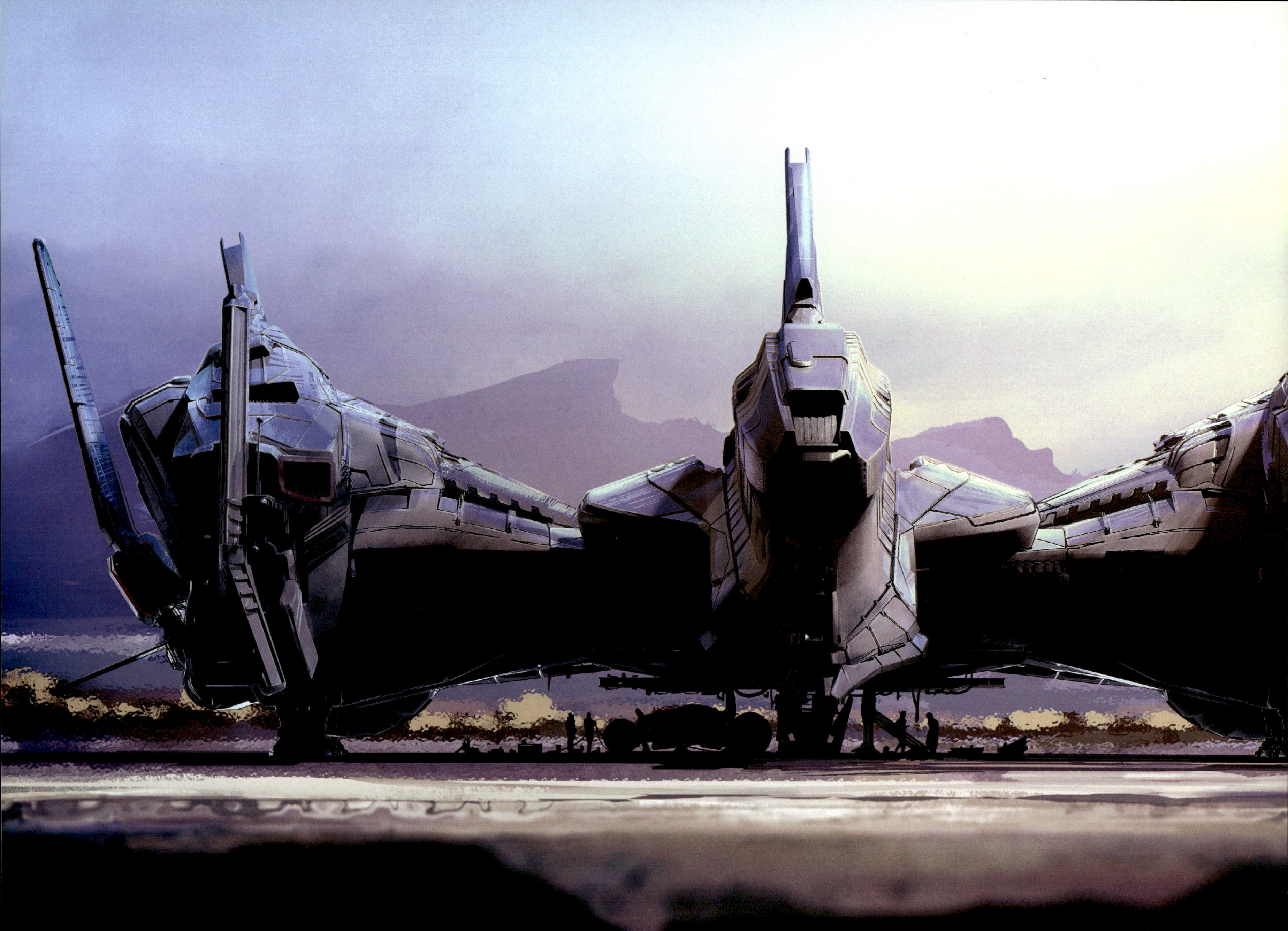

My thoughts went immediately to Asha - what she had tried to do for me. Her face, clean of the scars life outside the Oasis normally left on those of us who spent our short lives searching for water. Was she now hurt? Would they all soon face life wandering the badlands?

We headed back. INC had returned to his old self.

"Do you think there was an accident?" "What could do that kind of damage?" "Do you think it was a dispute?" "The female said there were others like her. Could they have caused this?"

I think he eventually got the hint by my repeatedly responding, "I don't know, INC."

From the outside of the Oasis, everything seemed calm. Only small threads of smoke wafted upward. The only real evidence of damage was a few holes to one of the external walls, and they were blasted out from the inside.

Any other damage was hidden within the walls.

I peered in through one of the large holes. Through all the structures and damage, it was hard to make anything out. One thing for sure, there was plenty of chaos.

"We're going in," I said. "Keep low and close to me."

"Should we …" INC asked.

" … and quiet," I added.

We entered through one of the large, blasted holes in the wall, then snuck from building to building, hiding in a burnt-out structure.

We could finally see to the large, open space that separated the living areas from the Citadel.

The smoldering wreckage of one of the enormous guardians lay on the ground.

"Who are they?" INC asked in his best "whisper."

"They're definitely not from around here," I replied.

Several men - well-armored men like I'd never seen before - seemed to be salvaging the guardian for parts.

A hundred yards away, citizens of the Oasis yelled at them, clearly dismayed. Others were busy repairing buildings and homes. There was an air of confusion, as if their world had been turned upside down.

"Where did they come from?" INC asked.

"I'm guessing that thing right there."

There it rested, huge and magnificent, a spacecraft I would soon come to intimately know as: the Widows Revenge.

It was the largest flying ship I had ever seen. I've seen a few in my life, usually capable of carrying no more than three people, and for short distances, at that. This was huge, capable of carrying at least a couple dozen people, and cargo, to boot.

THE BOOK OF LANDIS 57

THE STORY OF INC

Suddenly, I was nabbed from behind by two guards.

INC grabbed one of them and flung him several feet. He was about to clobber the second one when I heard a voice behind me whisper my name.

"Calm your big friend down," Graton said. "Now, let's get indoors."

He led us to the rear door of a large structure.

"Can you be trusted?" Graton asked. "Because this is my home."

I looked at him and, with all sincerity, nodded.

"Me, too," INC added.

"Um … alright," Graton replied.

I had never seen a home this large, or with so many luxuries. Nothing like this had ever been seen outside the Oasis. Furniture with padding and white linens, a roof that was solid and without holes.

Then I saw her through an open door, working in the family garden. I was so happy to lay eyes on her again.

"Hi," I said.

She turned toward me, surprised not only to see that I had been allowed to return, but that I had been allowed in a cleric's home.

Around her neck hung a thick, metal ring with a heavy chain. At the end of the chain was a wooden cup with an intentionally large hole in the bottom.

This, I assume, was the "mild" punishment for stealing water.

Asha paused, and then said a tentative, "Hello." Angry and confused, she looked to her father for clarity.

He met her gaze with a look of determination. "Desperate times call for desperate measures."

For a man as stern and resolute as he was, he looked shaken and unsure.

He then turned to me and said, "We have little time."

The strangers had arrived late in the afternoon after we left. Their large ship landed within the walls of the Oasis. Most citizens hid, terrified, in their dwellings, having never seen a ship so large, let alone with the ability to leave the atmosphere.

"We were generous hosts," Graton explained, "welcoming even. But the weapons on their hips sent a clear message that we would be easily outgunned."

A tall, bearded man broke away from the rest of the pirates, and approached Graton. He identified himself as the captain of the vessel, Sturges.

THE BOOK OF LANDIS 59

"They professed they were here for one thing, trade," he continued. "According to the captain, they had medicine and technology to trade. Fair and simple. Or so he claimed."

The problem was with what they wanted in exchange.

"I informed them in the strongest possible terms, they would never get what they wanted. I offered them the best in handmade garments, jewelry and crops," Graton continued. "The man smirked at me. His eyes belittled me and my offer."

What they wanted rested within the holiest of locations.

"That's when they openly mocked and challenged the Creators," he said.

In a show of strength, Sturges approached the Citadel, activating the large statue that began to attack the pirates. With a short but intense battle, they had more than enough firepower to finally stop it, and clearly enough to stop any attack from the citizens.

"That is why we need your help," Graton said.

"Our help?" I asked. "How? Why me?"

Graton was convinced that since I was from the badlands, I would clearly know how to fight. After all, we were all primitives who did nothing but wage war and kill over water.

It seemed impossible. I knew nothing of war, and if the pirates could take out one of the guardians, we didn't stand a chance.

I could see Asha watching from the shadows, tearing up as she listened to our conversation. Her eyes shot daggers at me. Eyes I couldn't resist, no matter how much venom they threw my way.

I never let on that I had no idea what I was doing, but I needed to make things right with Asha.

"Take me to your armory," I told them.

I agreed I would help them, on one condition: I got a guaranteed spot at the end, and that included INC and the small cargo he was carrying, plus a dwelling that would house us all, and water for two.

At this point, he probably would have agreed to anything.

And one last thing, I told him.

"You will suspend Asha's punishment, indefinitely," I said.

For a moment, just a moment, her eyes softened, and she didn't hate me quite as much.

At nightfall, we covertly made our way across the Oasis to the opposite side of the settlement, where they kept a few weapons. We tried recruiting as many men as possible, but most were too scared, or dismayed that what they thought was divine was so easily defeated by men with weapons.

It didn't help things that there was so much tension between Asha and Graton. She never acknowledged a word he said to her, and often mumbled something contrary to herself whenever Graton spoke.

I tried to keep them focused on the task at hand.

"How do you know, with all the chaos, there wasn't a run for weapons?" I asked.

"We would have heard," Graton said. "Trust me, it's secure."

When we arrived at the armory, an elderly woman sat calmly doing needlework in front of the door.

"This was your big idea of a secure weapons cache?" I asked.

She put her needlework aside and said, "I'm the only midwife around, so you want a gun or a baby, you gotta come to me." She said, "I protect the weapons. Expectant fathers protect me."

While the armory's weapons were intact - a few dozen rifles, spears and axes - they were sadly inadequate compared to the pirates' advanced weapons and blasters.

We desperately tried to formulate a strategy. No matter what angle we tried, or tactic we used, we were outgunned. I told him the best tactic was probably negotiation.

The little old woman gave me a small grin and a nod. Graton would have none of it.

Suddenly, a panicked man approached, and pounded on the armory door.

"They're starting!" he cried.

Although they were on the far side of the Citadel, we could hear the blasters of the ship striking the outer walls of the huge tower. The sound was deafening.

THE BOOK OF LANDIS

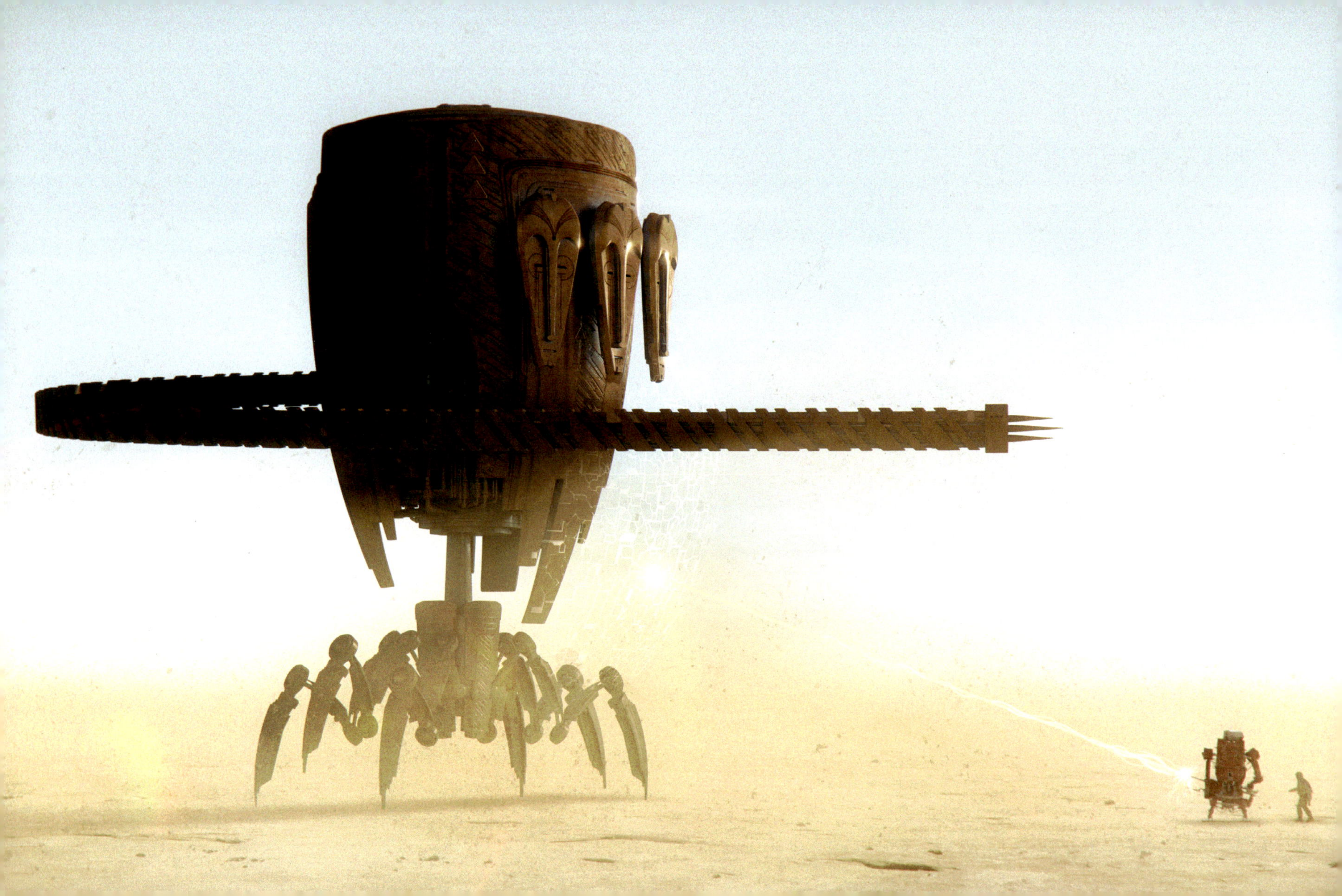

We ran out into the open, and that's when we noticed - the pirates' attack on the building had awoken the statue nearest us. It erupted from the ground, and set its gaze on us. People fled as the huge machine began its attack.

I fired my rifle, only to see the bullets bounce off its thick, metal shell.

The thing was fast, and I was not about to outrun it. It smashed the ground all around me.

"Get out of here!" I yelled at INC. As usual, he wouldn't listen.

Before I could even blink, a bright plasma arc shot over my head, striking the guardian in the chest. It was only stunned at first, and then went directly for INC.

Evidently, that night he wasn't just cleaning his plasma welder, he was turning it into a makeshift weapon.

INC stood his ground, and unleashed another stream of glowing plasma, ripping through one of the attacking machine's arms. It staggered, then nearly fell on top of INC, who didn't flinch.

"Oops. I should turn down the oxygen component next time," INC said. "I didn't mean to kill it."

"No," I said, "you did good."

He was hearing a much different message from Graton, who was beside himself with grief and rage. To him, we had killed a guardian of the temple - an angel.

It was strange how the guardian fell. It almost seemed human in its collapse, struggling to stay up. Did the thing actually feel? It seemed impossible, but then again, my own bot had been doing strange, even humanlike things, much to my surprise.

Then, after a moment, the huge bot began to twitch and slowly rose. This thing was not done with us.

INC took aim as his weapon recharged.

"Put your weapon down!" Graton frantically yelled. "You've hurt a guardian."

INC looked at Graton, then me.

I nodded that he should listen to Graton. He seemed to listen for a moment, then quickly raised the weapon.

"Our lives won't be determined by a condescending lunatic," INC replied.

My gut wrenched hearing my own words coming out of him.

Before he could fire, three rockets from the pirates hit the guardian in the head, finally taking it down.

Graton was inconsolable. Two guardians dead, and the crushing sound of the Citadel being assaulted. In spite of her anger, Asha tried her best to comfort him, but her words fell on deaf ears.

The cleric fell to his knees in despair at watching the holy guardians he had loved and respected his whole life, the protectors of this sacred structure which had only done good for him and his people, fall to corrupt, thieving humans.

On the other side of the Citadel, the pirates fired into the walls of the building with their cannons.

"I'll do everything I can to stop them," I assured Asha. "They'll listen to reason - how these people need the water it provides. I'll make it right."

She scooped up her now-unresponsive father, and looked at me with tears in her eyes.

She whispered to me. I don't know the exact words she spoke, but I'm quite certain they ended with, "I'm not sure I want you to."

INC and I ran as quickly as we could, but it seemed to take forever to cover the huge distance along the massive building.

We passed terrified citizens who fled in panic as their world seemed to crumble around them.

When we arrived, the Widows Revenge hovered in the air, its giant engines roaring and powerful cannons blasting their way into the side of the Citadel.

I'll admit, it was something to behold. The ship just seemed magical. So large, but it seemed to float there. Not to mention the firepower it wielded.

And it was beautiful, even while it pounded the walls of the temple.

It took me a moment to gather myself. I looked to INC, who returned the look and held up his welder as if to say - I'm ready to fire.

At that point, it was too late. The cannons stopped, and once the smoke cleared, it revealed a giant hole in the northern wall.

The Widows Revenge descended to the ground, and the captain emerged on the boarding ramp with a cocky sense of victory.

INC immediately aimed his welder at him. Captain Sturges seemed unfazed, almost charmed by INC's actions.

"Rumor has it you two nearly took down a Mech Sentry by yourselves?" he said. "Impressive."

I could hear the hum of INC charging up his weapon. I actually got a bit worried. I've never heard of a bot getting "mad," or being passionate about anything. INC, in the limited time he had been with me, never did anything out of turn, or without my express permission. Was he acting on his own, or because, through me, he thought this was how humans dealt with their problems?

THE BOOK OF LANDIS

Either way, here he was, his weapon raised and powered up, aimed at a human. His gaze was unflinching and focused.

"You're feisty, aren't you?" Sturges said to INC.

I put my hand on INC's arm, looked him in the eyes, and gently shook my head, no. He seemed to suddenly realize how he was behaving, and lowered his weapon. His demeanor was apologetic toward me, but definitely not toward the captain.

Pirates quickly started to pile into the hole that had been blasted into the Citadel.

"You seem smart, and if you're willing and able to take on one of those sentries, you certainly can't be one of them," the captain said, a grin growing on his face. "Want to come see what's inside?"

He could sense my reluctance.

"Once you see inside, not only will you understand my point of view," he said, "but maybe you'll talk some sense into these folks."

We approached the enormous, smoldering hole. I turned back to see citizens looking on in horror, many in tears.

In the darkness of the Citadel, the only light came from the bright flashlights used by the pirates. From what I could see, this clearly wasn't, as the clerics described, golden cathedral halls built to house the angels. This was the interior of a giant machine. A still-functioning one, at that.

"This isn't the only one, either," Sturges said. "These things litter the galaxy, but this is the first inhabited planet we've found one on.

"We've never seen who made them," he continued, "but then again, we've done everything to avoid them."

He explained how the sentries were there to simply guard against pirates and scavengers, who would always try to poach the advanced power sources and metals. This is what the pirates did: plunder these machines for the resources inside.

"Amazing, what does it do?" INC asked.

THE BOOK OF LANDIS

THE BOOK OF LANDIS

"No idea," Sturges replied. "Whatever these things did do, this one clearly stopped doing it a long time ago. But lucky for you good folks, the water harvesters kept working. Usually, the water's converted for energy."

Evidently, hundreds of these machines on a planet's surface would drain any world into a desert, given enough time. This one had been running longer than most, apparently. In fact, one of the literally millions of tanks had sprung a small leak, and this was the source of the Oasis' water.

"Your confused friends out there have been sipping from a leak when they could have been guzzling from a firehose if they just had the courage to take a look."

While the citizens of the Oasis wailed outside for their fallen god and defiled temple, INC seemed to almost be having a religious experience from the sheer size of the machines at work inside, the domain of the mechanical and non-human.

It was clear Sturges was taking a liking to INC.

"Now you seem like a handy type," he told INC. "How would you like a job?"

Unsure how to answer, INC looked at me.

"Okay, both of you," Sturges continued. "Could use a couple extra hands."

THE BOOK OF LANDIS

His offer was simple - help them get the job done and get out of there, and they would help us get the water flowing, and help with some technology and medical supplies. My job was to bring the locals and the clerics, namely Graton, around to what was best for their small community.

I figured, what choice did they really have? The damage was done to their "temple," but what was presenting itself was good - plenty of water. Maybe they could even finally open the gates. Maybe, finally, an end to the suffering.

INC returned his weapon back to its intended function, a welding gun, and went to work dismantling what was left of the second sentry.

The pirates seemed primarily interested in precious metals, rare minerals and random tech equipment. Nothing the Oasis couldn't live without.

"Let's find where your water's coming from," Sturges said.

The captain and I made our way up, deep inside the Citadel. We found the source of the leak. Water drizzled out continually from several of tons of massive tanks.

"It doesn't seem very … mystical," I said.

"No, but the good news is there's enough water in this thing for generations," he replied.

I immediately drank … and drank. I drank until my belly ached.

I let it shower over me until I was completely wet. Aside from my own sweat, I had never been completely wet before. This was one of the happiest days of my life.

I sent several of the pirates out with buckets filled to the brim to present as peace offerings to the locals. I said it was best if they made the offering instead of me. The captain agreed.

Sturges gave me some tools, and the rest of the day was filled with stories of his exploits from around the galaxy as we harvested small components. I listened to tales of aliens, shimmering, wealthy cities and bizarre, water-covered worlds.

He delighted in his lifestyle, the freedom and discovery of finding new worlds and seeing the galaxy. I have to say, it was a life I would have never even thought possible. Living in a world of dust and dehydrated agony, you tend not to daydream much, let alone fantasize about galactic travel.

We went higher into the tower, and stood out on a large opening about midway up. I could see for miles, out toward the Coral Barrens, and the vast badlands that I had called home for so long.

THE BOOK OF LANDIS

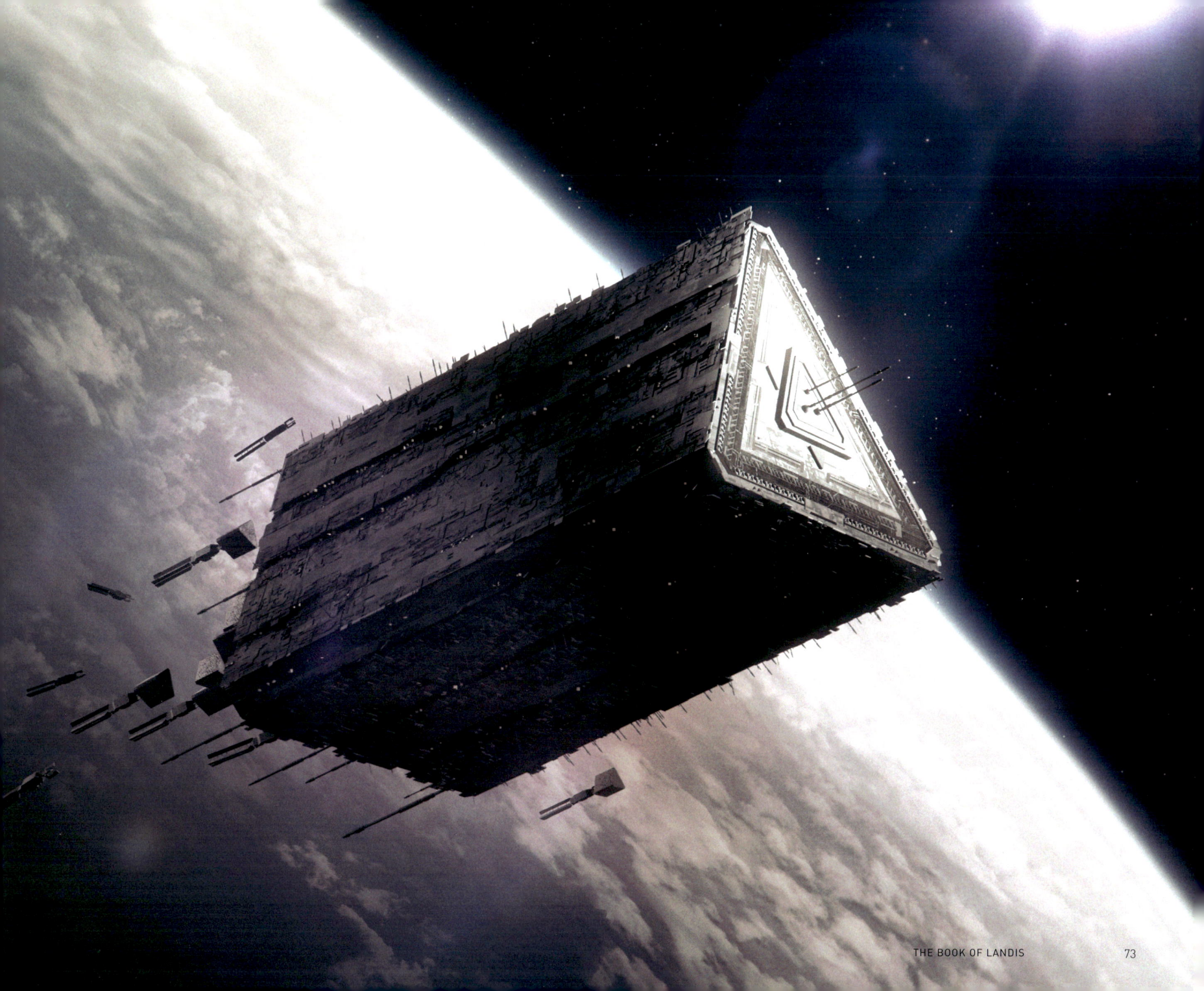

"It's a wonder any of you survived out there," Sturges said. "I'm sure you want more than that."

Sturges opened his pack. It was filled with tiny components, and bits and pieces of small, highly advanced alien technology.

"What's in this pack alone is more than enough to make this trip worthwhile," he said, pulling out a minute metallic cylinder. "Just this little sucker will make me more money than you've seen in your entire life on this dusty planetoid."

After a while, he sounded less like he was telling stories, and more like he was giving a sales pitch. But I had a promise to keep and a family to start, and with the new abundance of water, I was well on my way.

As we headed for the exit, I stopped by the leak again and had my fill. This was how it would be now, not just for us and the citizens of the Oasis, but for everyone.

INC was working away, disassembling what was left of the sentry. Pirates loaded the parts they wanted into the Widows Revenge.

THE BOOK OF LANDIS

THE STORY OF INC

I watched as they carried their cargo into the belly of the giant ship. I was dying to see the inside - the technology, the seduction of cruising across the galaxy.

Suddenly, there was a bang, and one of the pirates fell off the boarding ramp and onto the ground. He grasped his arm in pain.

"We're being ambushed!" yelled another pirate.

Bullets flew past our heads and onto the ground, then, just as quickly, stopped. Pirates drew their weapons, but couldn't spot the source of the shots.

Graton emerged from an angry mob that had gathered.

"We have you surrounded. Snipers have their sights on each of you," he said. "You will be put on trial for your crimes and punished according to the law."

Then he looked at me, his eyes filled with disgust.

This was my cue, to make peace. Once he saw the bounty inside, and that this building was nothing more than a giant machine, he would come around. It was a hard pill to swallow, but things would change now, and for the better.

I barely got a few words out before I was labeled the traitor. How could I help them, he asked. How could I kill one of the guardians? He said he made a mistake making a deal with me.

"I'm sorry," he declared, "but you and your armed bot can't be trusted."

Then, I realized how INC looked, his welder raised, standing over the remains of a fallen guardian bot. Even though it wasn't a functioning weapon anymore, that's not how it looked to Graton.

Before I had a chance to blink, before I could get a word out or plead my case, bullets flew through the air … and struck INC.

"No!" I yelled.

It took a moment for INC to react. I tried to convince myself that he hadn't taken any damage, but then fluids began trickling from him onto the ground.

I ran as quickly as I could toward him, when more shots rang out. The bullets ripped through INC. He didn't even have time to react. His head turned toward me and I was confident that I saw sadness in his eyes.

Then, he just fell to the ground.

In my panic, I ran to INC, oblivious to the firefight that was erupting around me.

The pirates fired their plasma guns amid lead bullets that struck everywhere. Lucky for the pirates, their armor protected them from most of the bullets flying their way.

All I really remember from that moment was my complete heartbreak, and that I was now the one asking all the questions.

"How do I fix you?!" I kept screaming at INC. "What are you leaking? What components are broken?"

He seemed confused, apologizing over and over, intermittently interrupting himself with that cold, digital voice that would say: Thirty seconds until this system or that system failure.

"Shut up and get to fixing yourself," I ordered.

Bullets were still zipping past our heads, but nothing could break my focus.

Then, anger took over. I yelled at him. Why didn't he hide? Why didn't he move? I told him he was useless. He had one function, and he failed.

"You're right," he said. "I'm sorry."

Then, he said it. Well, not him, but the rudimentary computer part of him. Without feeling, without emotion or urgency, "Three minutes until core incubation system failure."

INC looked at me, momentarily realizing what he had just said … then, his heartbroken eyes went dim.

I wasn't thinking right. Not in my right mind. I marched over to the fallen pirate who nursed his bleeding arm, and grabbed his plasma pistol.

I took aim and fired. Fired right at his head, but my shot just missed Graton by inches. I kept firing, but with my blurred vision, I just kept missing my target.

Graton quickly took cover. Bullets flew at us from every direction. The pirates kept returning fire, but were never able to spot their targets.

"Get to the ship," Sturges commanded. "Fire up the engines."

THE BOOK OF LANDIS

They had gotten what they needed, and what they didn't need was another firefight.

Time seemed to move in slow motion. I quietly stood there as the bullets zipped past me. Pirates fired back blindly as they ran for their ship.

As the last one boarded, the engines rumbled the ground, and the ramp began to retract.

I looked at INC one last time. He was motionless. Stupid, simple bastard. I warned him every time to hide, to always take cover. But he never listened. Now, I was paying the price.

From the boarding ramp, I heard Sturges call my name.

I gained my bearings as the bullets flew past me. I charged for the ship, and jumped onto the boarding ramp.

"Grab hold of something," Sturges said. "It's going to get bumpy."

Everything vibrated, and there was this low, rumbling hum. As the ship banked and accelerated, I found myself crashing to the floor.

I rushed to a porthole nearby to watch the ground falling away. I could hear small dings as bullets bounced off the hull of the ship. The few men with rifles on the ground emerged from their hiding places to fire their last, futile shots at the vessel.

I made my way to the bridge, where Sturges and his crew set their course to leave the planet.

I looked out the main viewport to see us flying in mere moments across the landscape that took me weeks to cross. We ascended toward the blue sky, then upward as it turned dark and filled with stars.

Sturges finally shifted his attention to me.

"There is nothing there for you now. In fact, I'm pretty sure they'd kill you," he said. "Be glad we got out of there when we did."

I looked to the massive view screen.

THE BOOK OF LANDIS   81

"Your future's out there," he continued. "You owe us work on three jobs, then you're free to go. That's how it works here. No one gets free passage … But I hope you stay."

Out the viewport, the stars grew closer and brighter. Soon galaxies, then nebula, revealed themselves.

With INC gone, as well as my chance for a family, the view was empty, cold and without meaning. I guess in that moment, so was I. It wasn't INC who failed in his task, but me. I was the one who made the promise.

I was suited up with their standard armor. A couple of them laughed at me because I had a few of the pieces on backward. They quickly gave me duties, simple chores to pick up the slack for the wounded.

I just swallowed the pain inside and tried to bury myself in the work, attempting to focus on the worlds to explore ahead of me.

I would see distant worlds, new civilizations and never want for water again. But I was doing it alone, and I had never been alone before.

I couldn't get the vision out of my head of INC resting where he feared the most, on top of a pile of discarded bots, one of many, just rusting, alone and forgotten.

With my stomach churning, it was all the more difficult to distract myself.

I was still trying to get my footing on a spacecraft, my "space legs," as they said. The constant vibration of the engines, the synthetic gravity that was, well, anything but consistent. I was definitely not ready for what was about to happen next.

I'm not sure what initially hit the hull, but it sent most of us flying. Alarms sounded throughout the ship.

Everyone scrambled to their positions. I just did everything in my power not to throw up.

The ship moved and banked, spun and dove. I held on for dear life and tried to keep down my lunch.

"Divert excess power to rear shields," Sturges ordered.

Once on the bridge, I looked out the view screen to see that we were flying past what would seem indescribable.

"What the hell is that thing?" I asked.

Up until that moment, the Citadel was the biggest structure I had ever seen. This dwarfed it. It was a hundred times the size of the Citadel, easily.

The captain didn't answer, but the look on his face told me this was not good.

"Prep countermeasures," Sturges said. "Arm missiles."

Small, what I interpreted as probes, launched from the massive ship and came right for us. We did our best to gain distance, but the probes kept up. The gunners blasted them left and right.

"Do NOT let them scan this ship!" Sturges ordered.

For a moment, I imagined if INC was there. He would just be barraging the captain with questions: "Who are they?" "Why is their ship so big?" "What's this lever do?"

In the middle of this tense moment, they must have thought it odd that I had a small smile on my face. It quickly left me when my stomach dropped as the ship suddenly banked hard left.

THE BOOK OF LANDIS

THE STORY OF INC

THE BOOK OF LANDIS

We were now heading straight for the mothership, hugging it as dangerously close as possible, sending the remaining probe smashing back into the huge ship that had launched it.

When we finally made our way clear of the enemy vessel, I was a sad, sick mess.

Relieved, I looked to the captain, who was anything but.

"That was some impressive flying. Not that I really have a point of reference. It could have been some of the worst, for all I know," I said. "Why didn't you want them to scan this ship?"

He was hesitant, but finally answered.

"Because we're carrying their goods," he said. "Stolen goods."

It took me a moment to put two and two together.

"What? So they're coming after us? How are we going to outrun that thing?"

"They're not after us … yet. They're on a different trajectory. We've got plenty of time to gain some distance," he said, but his mood didn't improve.

"Wait, what trajectory is it on? Where is it going?" I asked, but I already knew the answer.

"We must have set off an alarm or something," he replied.

He tried to justify what happened. Those towers were never on inhabited planets. Never. All the fighting must have triggered an alarm, or some kind of beacon.

He had no idea what was going to happen once they arrived, or how they would treat the locals.

For me, it was settled then. We had to head back. We had to warn the people at the Oasis.

"No. I'm not committing suicide for a backward people who won't listen to reason," he said. "With the size of that ship, the technology in those towers, those beings would annihilate us. Not to mention, those people you want to save killed your bot and tried to kill you."

"I have to … I have to believe." I never imagined those words would come out of my mouth, but here they were. "I have to believe that there are good people still there," I said, "innocent people."

Of course, my thoughts went to Asha. She didn't deserve to be left there.

For the captain, that was the end of the conversation. He set course for some trading post on a nearby system to dump the goods as quickly as possible and then put as much distance between us and those beings as he could.

"You're a coward," I said.

If you ever need to know the magic words to push a pirate captain's buttons, those are the ones.

Before I could blink, he was right in my face. His eyes were intense and reminded me that he didn't have to save me, he did me a favor.

"I stopped you from killing that nut Graton, too, which would have made you a murderer," he said. "And all over some pet bot you had gotten overly attached to."

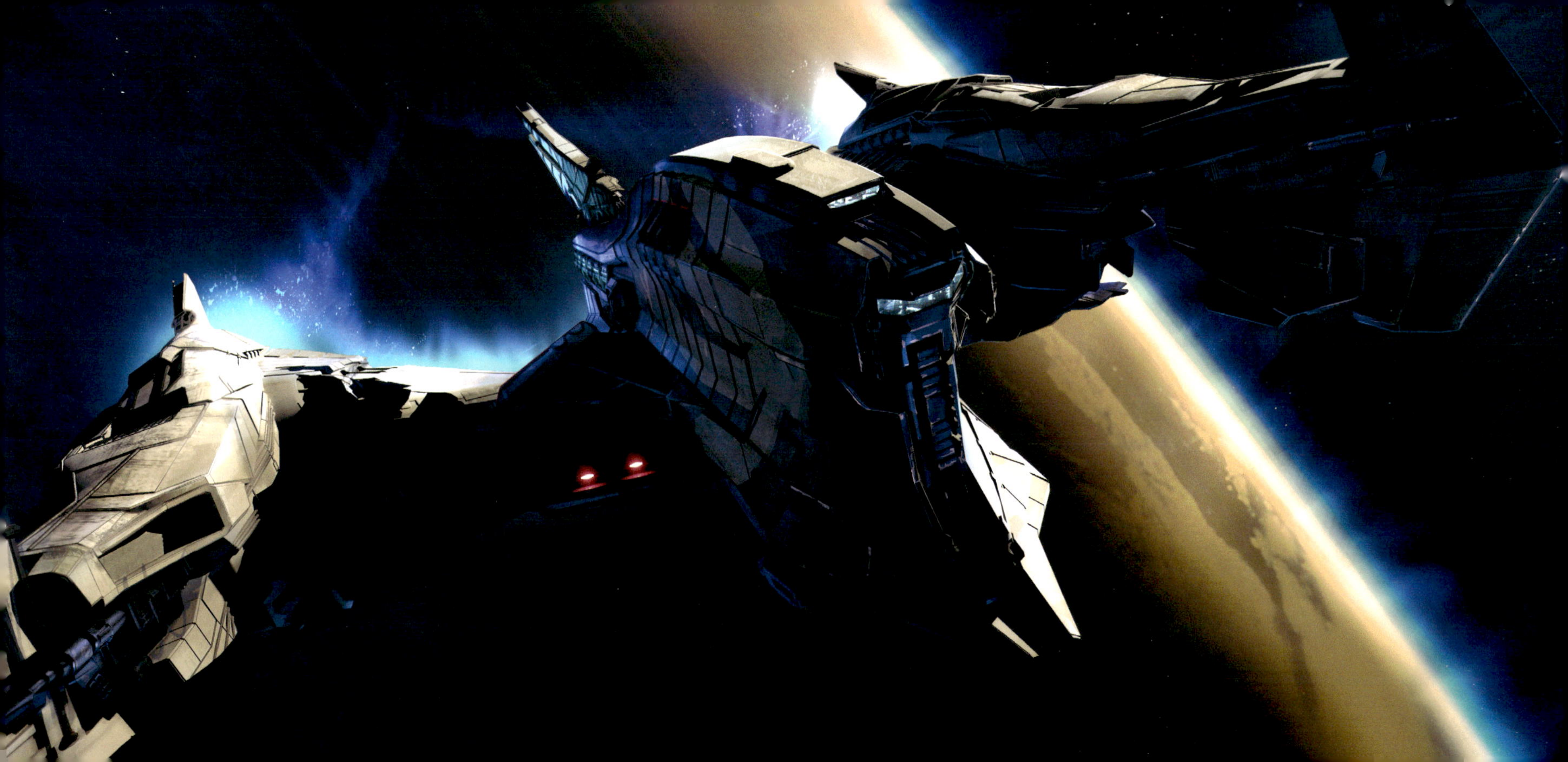

I made sure my initial punch landed squarely. I was probably only going to get one shot at it.

It fazed him for maybe half a second, just enough for me to tackle him to the ground. He put up an amazing fight, and even though I was still recovering from flight sickness, I held my own. When I finally got him pinned, he stopped fighting.

It helped that I had his own blaster aimed at his chest.

"You're the murderer," I said. "If you hadn't shown up, none of this would have happened. Those people's lives are on your head."

When I stood, I realized there were a dozen blasters aimed at me. I kept a firm grip on my weapon. If this was it, I was gonna take a few of them out with me.

"Put your weapons down," Sturges ordered.

He stood up and regained his dignity. He grabbed his weapon from my hand.

"He's taking the Orphan," he said. "If he wants to commit suicide, that's his choice."

They clearly weren't happy with the order, but put their weapons down.

"If I ever see your face again," Sturges said, "I'll kill you myself."

The "Orphan" was a small drop ship, possibly an escape pod, not sure. It could hold maybe three. I squeezed into the single pilot's seat.

I stared out the tiny viewport toward the planet in the distance. It even looked dry and desolate from space, but it was the place that made me.

What kind of person had I been? I was INC's only example of how people should behave, and I failed at that, badly. It was time to change that and make a difference, even if they hated me, or wanted me dead.

They gave me a quick rundown on throttle, steering and breaking, but the Orphan was pretty much automated. I didn't have to do much. Enter in coordinates and the thing would fly me there on autopilot.

That wasn't good enough. I needed time, and I was going to punch this thing to its limits.

As soon as it detached, I switched into manual mode and went full throttle. I was moving faster than I had ever dreamed. At first, the planet seemed to move toward me rather slowly, but once I got close, it seemed to race at me at a startling rate. Clouds zipped past me, then mountains. I even clipped the peaks of ancient, towering coral.

In hindsight, I really should have switched back to autopilot for the landing, but I had been flying for eight whole minutes by then, and felt I was pretty experienced.

I hit the ground hard, with tremendous speed, sliding and digging deep into the dirt. I had really miscalculated my descent, and smashed through one of the outside walls and into the Oasis. I skidded, knocking down a few tents in the process, until I finally came to a stop near the Citadel.

When I realized I was lucky enough to still be in one piece, I thought, well that was stupid, but awesome.

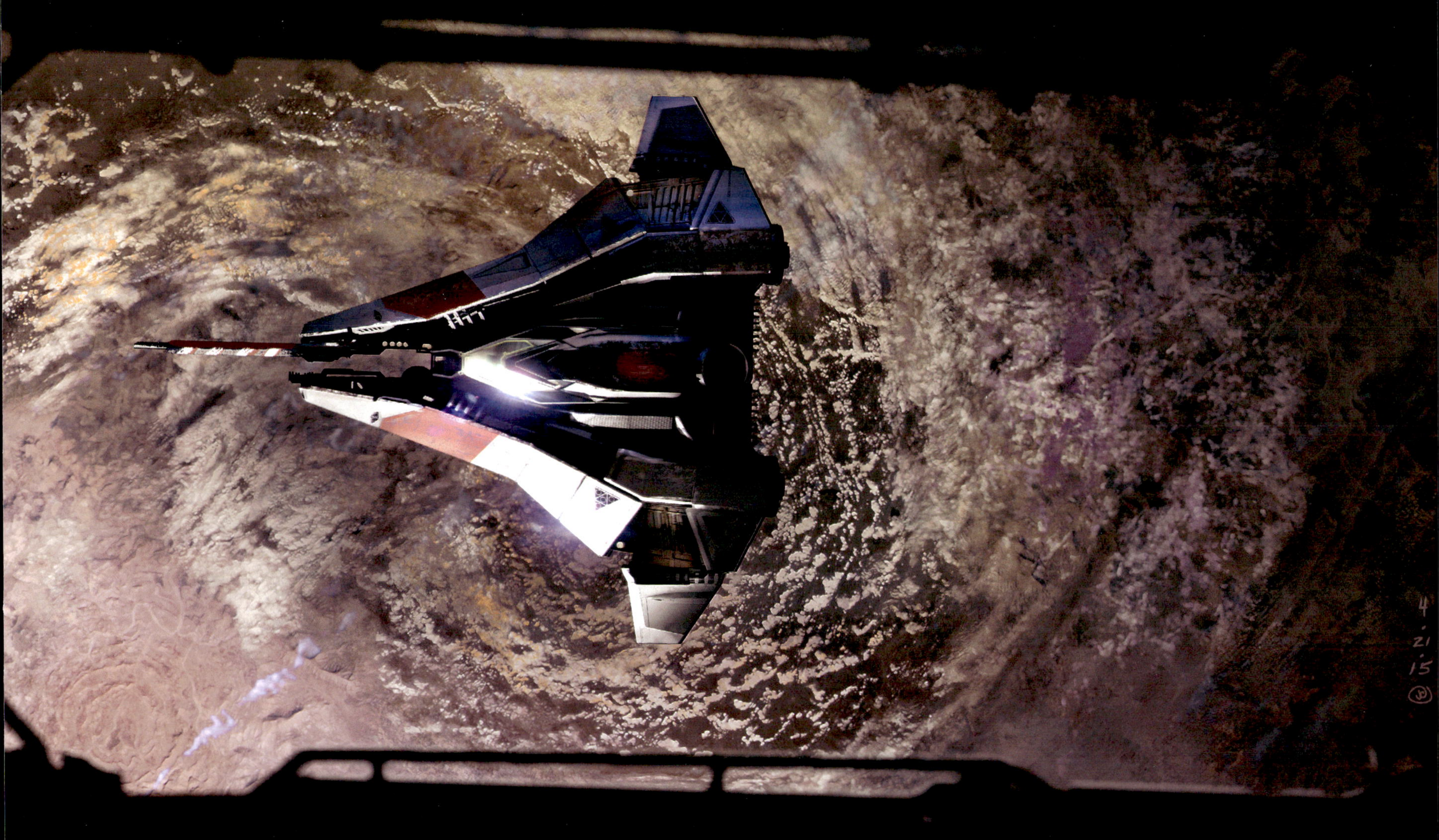
4.21.15

THE STORY OF INC

THE BOOK OF LANDIS

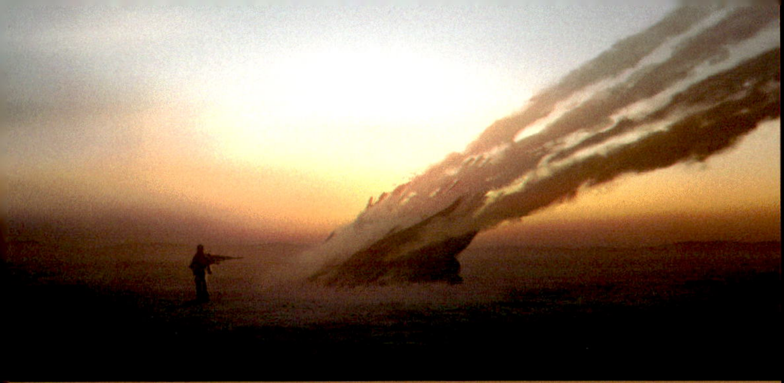
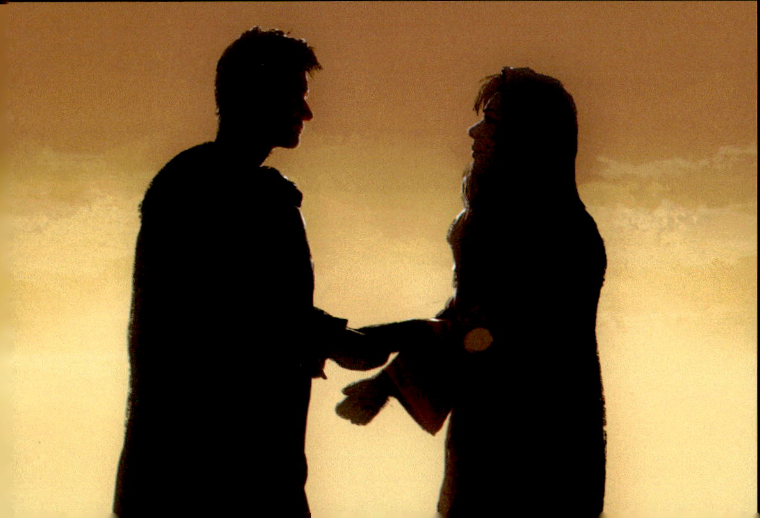
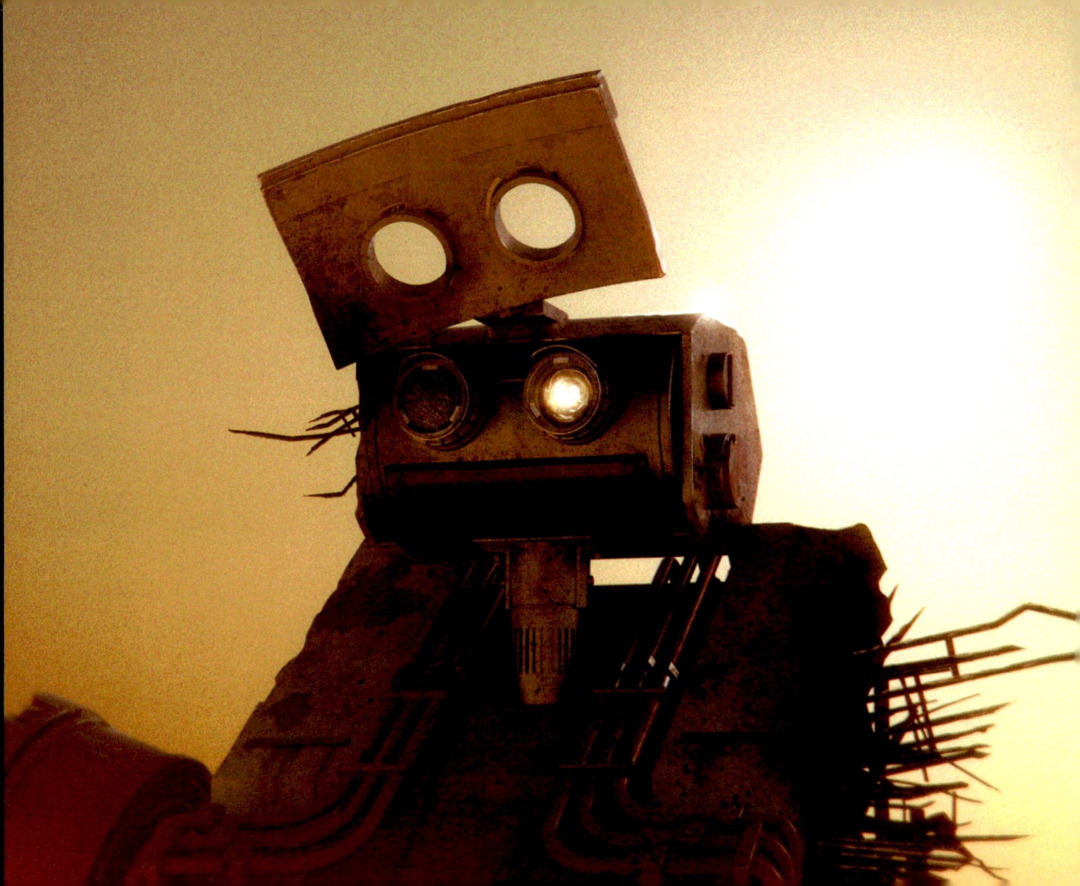

Chapter 04

OF FRIENDS AND ENEMIES

People quickly gathered around the cloud of dust and debris that engulfed my small ship. I took a deep breath, made sure my new armor was still in place under my cloak, and had easy access to the blaster on my hip should it turn ugly.

I knew if I just found Asha, she would believe me, and maybe even be able to convince the others she claimed "thought like her."

When I emerged from the dust cloud, most people ran, or just avoided me. I started grabbing anyone I could. I kept asking for Asha, which only startled them more, as if even mentioning her name would get them in trouble.

"We should get you indoors before you're spotted,"

from the armory.

Her small dwelling was cramped and modest. Almost no personal items of her own, but the tiny place was filled with everything she needed for helping new mothers through labor.

"I'm sorry about your friend," she said.

I tried not to get caught up in some sort of self pity. I quickly turned the focus to Asha.

"Things have taken a turn for the worse, I'm afraid," she replied.

After we had left, Asha and a small group of rebels confronted the clerics and their guards. Tired of their control of the city, control of the water and refusal to accept the new world that was appearing before them, they knew it was their time for action.

Asha and her group felt they had a right to know what secrets rested inside the heart of the Citadel.

Graton and his men would have none of it. All

hope of a peaceful resolution quickly vanished.

Despite Asha's efforts, a battle erupted. It didn't go well for the rebels.

"She's currently awaiting her punishment," the old woman said. "I fear the worst. Not just for her, but for all of us."

"Well," I said, "you're not going to like what I have to say next."

I told her about what was coming, and that everyone had to flee - abandon the only homes they knew and the safety of the walls of the Oasis.

She knew many would never leave, but she agreed our best option was to first get Asha, as she had built a following because of her heroism.

We found the few remaining supporters of Asha who were still willing to risk their lives to save her. None of them were real fond of the idea of having me in charge, but they didn't have much of a choice, and I had the biggest gun.

THE STORY OF INC

We quietly made our way to the detention center. There were several guards around the entrance - two brothers and a cousin, evidently. One of my men knew these guards. He had a plan, and ran off before we could stop him.

He walked up to the guards as if in a panic, and started pleading with them. Suddenly, all three guards rushed off in a hurry.

The entrance was now clear. According to the man, one of the brothers was expecting his first child any day. He just told him that the old woman was under attack by rebels at the armory. To say she was under attack was like saying his future child was under attack.

The cell block was dingy and dirty. Several of Asha's fellow rebels filled the cells. At the very end of the block, in her own cell, sat a battered and defeated Asha.

"Listen," I said. "I know you and your father are having a few … issues. But we've got bigger problems."

She just looked at me, a little surprised but definitely confused, as we opened the cells.

"They won," she said. "It's over."

"Not exactly," I replied. "It just got a lot more complicated."

On the news, she was quick to make her plans for escape routes and evacuation. She commanded her small band of rebels with surprising confidence.

She then stopped herself, and looked at me with some sadness.

"After you left, some of us temporarily patched your bot … He's carrying your baby?"

"Well, a frozen fertilized egg … yeah, still weird, I know," I said. "Where is he?"

"The Citadel," she said. "That bot never stopped asking questions. Was he like that with you?"

"You have no idea," I replied.

He did ask too many questions, including why his friend would leave him. But he believed the answer to that one was clear - I never saw him as a friend, just as a machine. A machine that had failed in its one and only task.

Suddenly, the sky went dark. We rushed outside to see the sky being overtaken by the huge ship arriving to reclaim the Citadel. It blotted out the sun, and its engine made a rumble that shook everything.

"Go," she said. "But get yourself out of there as soon as possible."

As I rushed off to find INC, Asha stopped me. "By the way, thanks for coming back for us… Now, go save your friend."

I made my way across the Oasis. People fled, and I had trouble making my way through the crowd that was rushing out as I was rushing in.

THE BOOK OF LANDIS   95

suddenly, I heard screams, and saw people being flung through the air. In their panic, everyone had started grabbing water wherever they could, and accidentally awoke the last Mech Sentry.

It was much taller than its two brothers, and as I ran straight for it, I hoped my blaster was enough to take care of it.

I quickly learned it wasn't. It slowed the sentry down at times, but not enough to stop it. I tried to keep it occupied as long as I could, allowing people to escape. It dawned on me that the last two times I faced one of these things, it was INC who saved me.

THE BOOK OF LANDIS

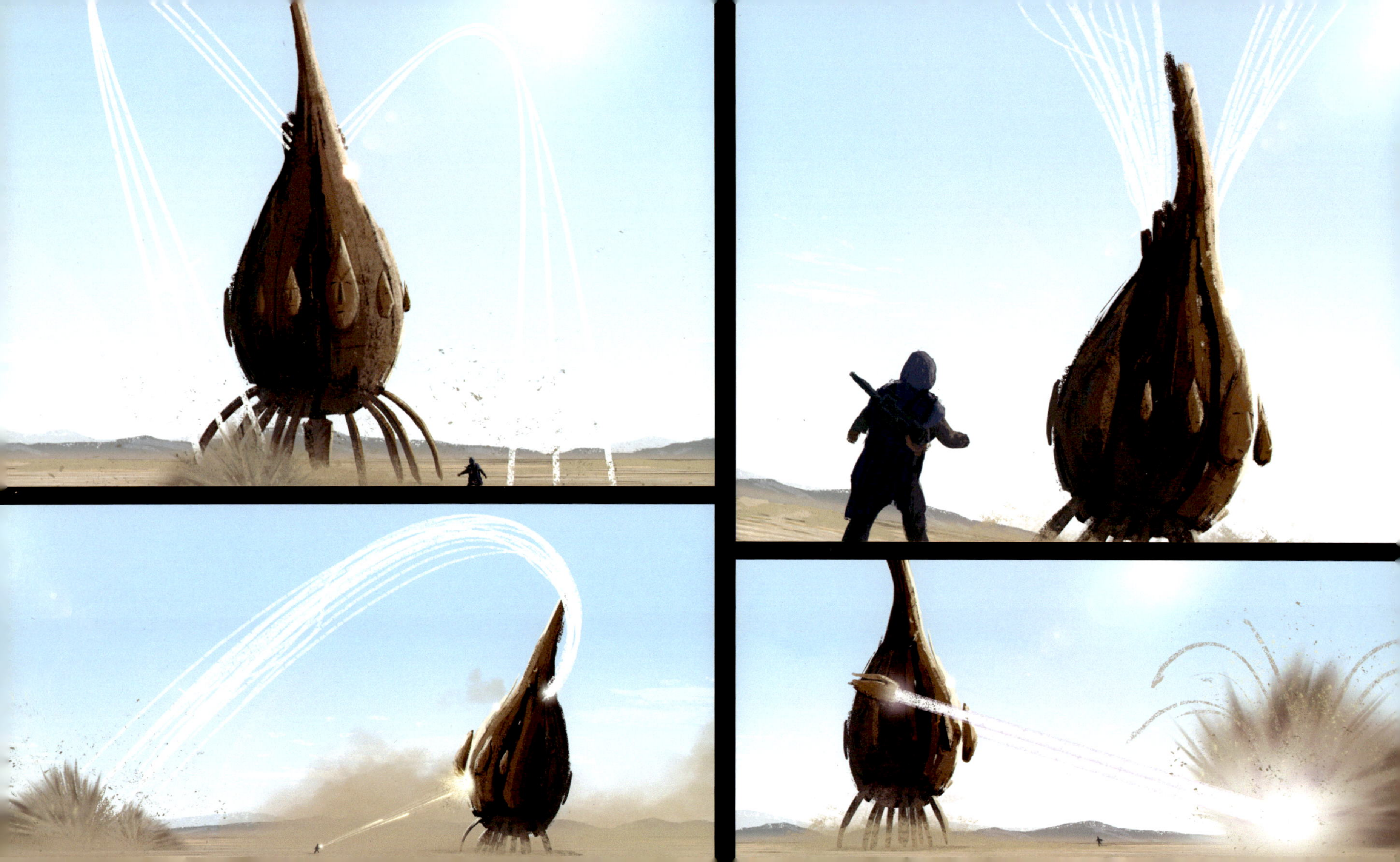

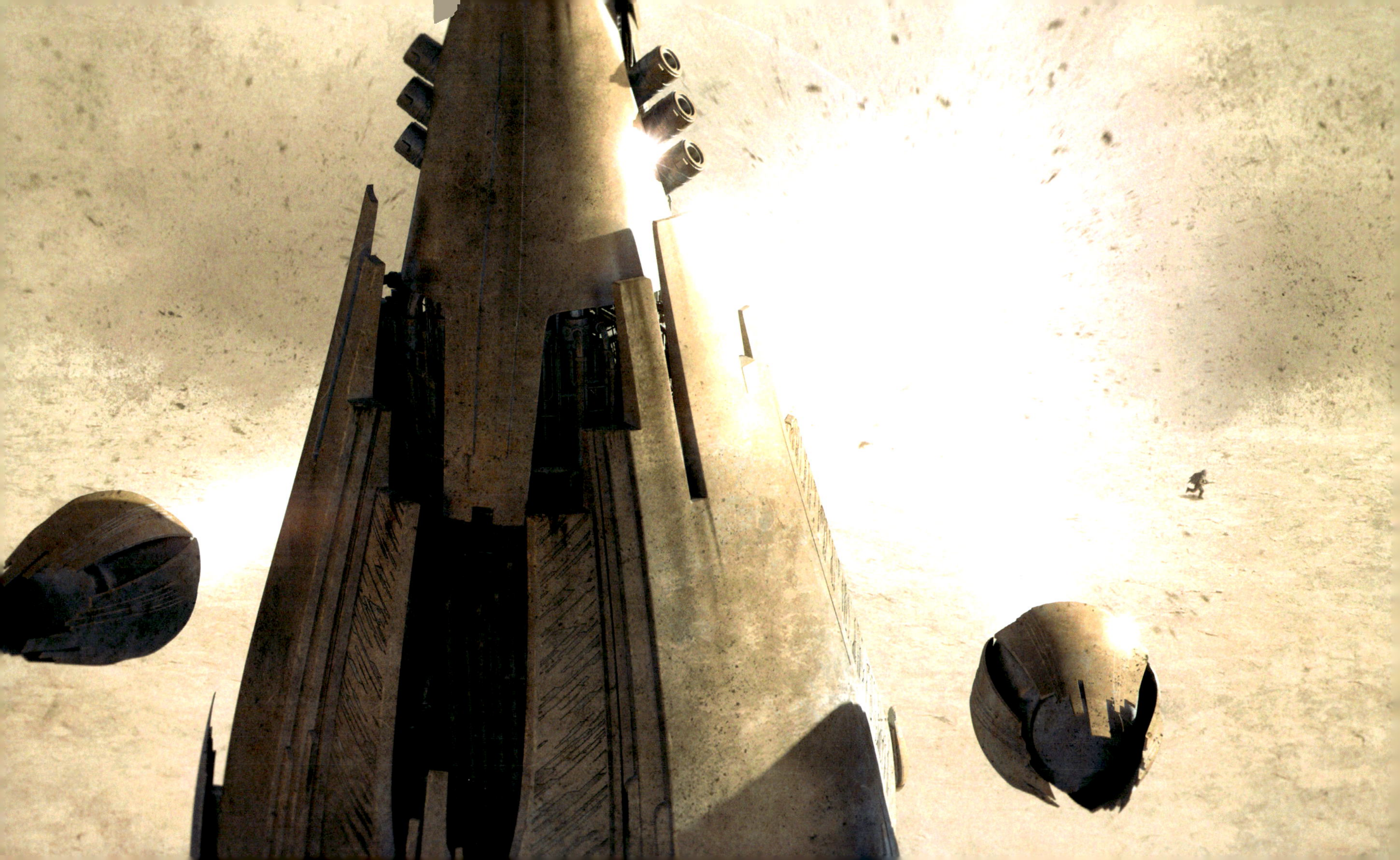

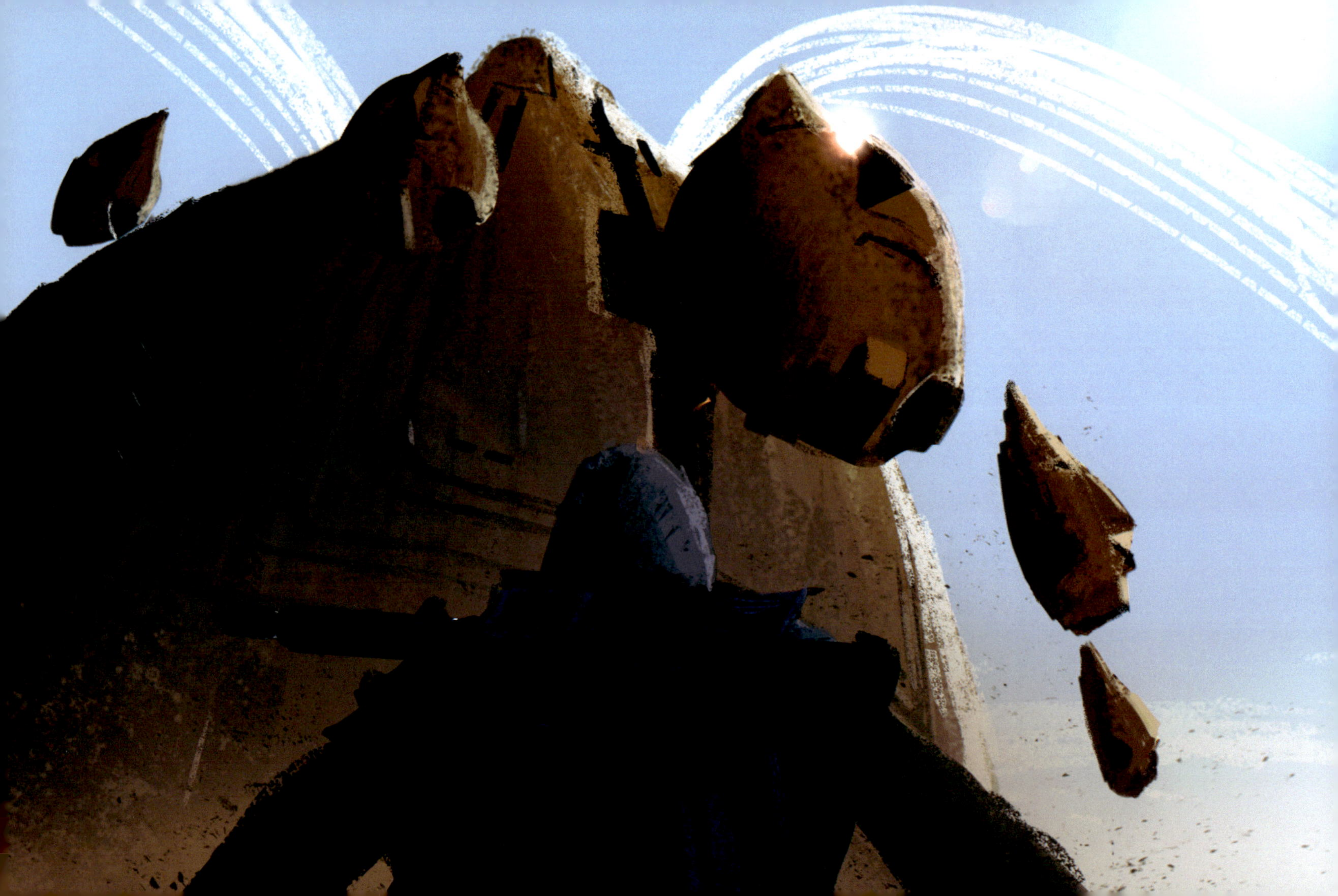

As it pounded me with its laser cannons, I searched in vain for any weak spot. At last, I managed to disable its cannons with some carefully placed shots to their core. But that wasn't the only trick up its sleeves. Next, the rockets came. Dust swirled in the air as the sentry razed the ground.

In a desperate ploy, I ran for cover to the only place the rockets couldn't reach, directly under the beast. But as before, I traded one danger for another. Its giant legs spun around, trying to crush me like an insect.

I stood there as the thing towered over me and wound up to deal its final blow, until it was distracted by something racing right toward it. A missile slammed straight into it.

It staggered back, and I ran for cover, but it was only momentarily deterred. It limped after me until it exploded into tiny pieces as two missiles from the Widows Revenge pounded into its chest.

I watched the ship zip over me and toward the front of the Oasis.

Asha was gathering people as quickly as she could among the chaos. They had to evacuate, but to where? How could she possibly get them a safe distance away? What was a safe distance?

She filtered them out the gates, trying to create groups and designate leaders, grabbing supplies and all the water they could carry.

She kept to herself her doubts that they would be able to get away before it was too late.

That's when she noticed something else in the sky, racing straight for her.

When I got to the hole in the Citadel, all the guards had fled. I was looking into the large, burnt-out blast hole, into the dark, cavernous interior of the Citadel. How would I ever find him inside that maze?

Then, I saw my answer. A small trail of fluid. It was irregular and sporadic, but a trail. Clearly, INC was having trouble, struggling with everything he had to make his way inside.

I rushed in, following the trail, calling his name.

What I didn't know was that Graton had learned of my return. He and a band of loyal guards quietly entered the Citadel moments after I did.

I followed the trail of fluid down corridors and walkways. It was a giant maze, designed for giants, and clearly INC was checking every corner to find parts, replacement fluids, whatever would work.

THE BOOK OF LANDIS

THE STORY OF INC

That's when I heard, off in the distance, the sound of a plasma welder. It bounced and echoed, only making it more difficult to pinpoint. Then, I finally spotted a distant light sparking. It flared and glowed. It had to be INC's welder.

Outside, the crowd rushed out the front gates of the Oasis, the huge mothership hovering in the sky over the Citadel behind them. Asha tried to keep order and move people as quickly as possible. Secretly, she had no idea how she would save all these people.

"We're a bit short on time," Captain Sturges' voice boomed from a loud speaker, "so let's get as many as we can in the cargo hold, and get them out of here."

Asha turned to see in the distance the Widows Revenge lowering its cargo door. She watched as the pirates dumped their cargo to make room for passengers.

She wrestled with whether to trust the captain as he made his way out of the ship.

"It's not first class, and there's no meal service," Sturges said, "but it might save your skins."

Asha nodded, and quickly steered people toward the ship.

Sturges watched as the deluge of people rushed his precious vessel. He was overheard whispering to himself, "Having a conscience is overrated."

Inside, I could feel the whole structure suddenly shake as if something was clamping onto the Citadel. The process had begun, and they were reclaiming what was theirs.

I quickly made my way over pipes, giant support structures and large mechanisms.

Then, I saw him … or what was left of him. He had not only scrounged parts from the Citadel, but had started to cannibalize his own. Next to him rested a welded-together cylindrical container that included Citadel parts, but mostly INC's inner workings. Steam rose from it, and it was clearly operating.

104 THE STORY OF INC

Chapter 05
A COLLISION OF CONSCIENCES

His belly was empty. Parts spilled onto the floor - wire and cut cables. Puddles of fluid lay around him.

Finding myself at a loss for words, I saw that he was clearly barely functioning, and fading in and out of awareness.

"I was unable to maintain the frozen embryo," he said. "I'm sorry."

"I know. It's not your fault," I said. "I'm sorry. I shouldn't have left you. I shouldn't have said those things to you…"

"In 38 weeks," he said, "you will be a father."

"What?" I replied.

"I'm sorry, I could not retrieve any additional liquid nitrogen, so I began the incubation process," he said. "I had to improvise a bit."

I could hear the sounds of the huge ship docking with the Citadel above us. Suddenly, lights began powering on through the structure.

I tried to get him to tell me how to fix him, but he only replied with instructions on the incubation process: every week do this, every two weeks do that, how much water it required. I told him, trust me, I knew the process, to just shut up and listen. I didn't want to lose him again. I needed him.

"Like friends?" he asked.

"Yes, like … like the best of friends," I said. "Now stop asking goddamn questions, and tell me how to fix you."

That's when what felt like a sledge hammer slammed into my back and sent me to the ground hard.

With whatever strength he had left, INC pulled me close and tried to shield me.

I looked up to see about half a dozen men on catwalks, perched on pipes, and lurking in the corners. All had rifles trained on us. Lucky the first bullet had been stopped by my armor.

Graton emerged from the shadows.

"I'm guessing you didn't mend your relationship with the cleric," INC said.

"Not exactly," I replied.

Graton seethed. "I will not allow those who steal and defile the temple to share the same ground with the Creators. Only those who are worthy."

The men cocked their rifles.

"And I thought you were quick to violence …" INC whispered. "I apologize."

"Um, thanks, I think," I replied.

Above us, we could hear the sounds of moving metal, giant shield doors opening on top of the Citadel.

The cleric looked up toward the sound, and smiled. For him, this was the moment he had waited for his whole life - to meet the Creators.

He then raised his hand. The men took aim at INC and me.

"I'm sorry," he said, "but this must be."

Suddenly, a voice commanded, "Tell your men to drop their weapons."

Asha's voice never sounded so good.

Graton demanded she show herself. She refused, but tried to make peace. She tried reason, saying he had a responsibility: It was time to evacuate his people.

The building began to rumble, and something large was descending into it. Suddenly, this was real. This was happening. Whoever or whatever had created this thing was making its way toward us.

Asha finally emerged from the shadows to plead her case. "Father, it's time to leave. Please."

He looked at her with tortured eyes. "Why, Asha? All I tried to do was protect us. To prove us worthy. You've tried to tear it all down."

From the rafters, Graton's men began to yell at her, calling her a traitor. They shouted threats and insults.

Graton demanded discipline from the soldiers, and the air grew tense. Despite her betrayal, she was still his daughter, and they would show respect. The soldiers raised their weapons. Asha's rebels raised theirs.

Suddenly, shots rang out. One hit Asha in the shoulder. Graton jumped in front of his only child to block any bullets that came her way. That's when a bullet intended for her landed squarely in his back.

Around them, a short gun battle ensued. Most of the loyal guards were killed, or fled as it became clear they didn't stand a chance against Asha's well-hidden rebels.

INC and I just kept as low as we could.

Graton tried to stand tall and proud as long as possible, but he finally collapsed to the ground, as Asha loudly demanded a ceasefire.

She bent down and gently rolled him over. Blood just started to trickle from his mouth. He put his hand on her cheek and spoke with love in his eyes, but the words were too faint to hear.

Then, everything seemed to go quiet.

He turned his head and looked beyond her, and smiled at what he saw.

"Beautiful…" he managed to get out.

THE BOOK OF LANDIS 107

THE STORY OF INC

Behind her, to our shock, was the Creator. An alien stood over us, sixty feet tall, unlike anything we could have imagined. A tall, elegant-looking being with a slender build.

When Asha turned back to her father, his stare was blank and all life had left him. Her tears quickly turned to anger. She beat on his chest with her fists, asking why wouldn't he listen, why wouldn't he change?

The being watched us with curious amazement. Then, as if we were a mere distraction, went about his work. Machinery that had been off for centuries began to power up. Large, red lights blinked and the devices gave off a distinct electric hum.

As quietly as I could, I told Asha it was time to go. We had to get out now. The beings were taking back their machine, and us along with it.

Asha stood and turned toward the being.

"Why? Why did you put this here? Why did you take our water?" she demanded, picking up her gun and aiming it at the being.

It took a minute, but the being finally turned its attention to us. He looked at us with a bit of bewilderment, similar to how we would look at a squeaking mouse. What did these pests want, these simple creatures? He again turned back to his work.

Asha took aim and cocked her weapon. I regained my breath and, with my chest thumping, rushed over and took her to the ground, causing her shot to miss its target.

The shot ruptured a pipe, sending steam everywhere.

"We have people to save," I reminded her. "That's why we did this, right? Now, let's get out of here."

She wiped the tears from her eyes, and found her focus.

But the being had turned his attention to us. He bent down, and took a closer look.

We just held still, terrified. Maybe if we don't move, it won't crush us, I thought.

The alien then fiddled with the rifle that lay on the ground. It examined it, then looked to us, then to the rifle, then back at us.

It wasn't angry, but what I assumed was … impressed. Like the little mouse had just used a power tool. It slowly rose and returned to its work.

Asha ordered the rebels to evacuate.

"INC, we have to go," I said. "Get up!"

He just looked at me, then at the being.

"I want to speak with the Creator," he said. "I have so many questions."

"Why am I not surprised?" I said. "They are just beings like any other."

"How do you know?" he asked. "You created me. Maybe they created you."

In hindsight, he was right. I knew nothing of the beings - who they were, what they were doing. They were lightyears ahead of us in so many ways, and probably more ancient than we could even grasp.

But in that moment, I was more interested in survival. I turned to Asha, who gave her father a gentle kiss before she rose.

I grabbed INC's hand.

"INC," I said, "you're gonna have to do most of the work here." I yelled, "INC, pay attention!"

When I looked at his face, he was gone. I could hear what was left of his system slowly fry and burn, the smell of charred circuits and metal.

The small incubator he had constructed began to beep. I was in complete shock. Luckily, Asha quickly unplugged its cord from INC.

He had used every ounce of power he had, overworking his entire system to keep the incubator running as long as he could, knowing it would eventually fry everything in him.

"We need to get this to a power source if you want to save your child," she said.

At first, I didn't hear her. I just stared at him. His lifeless eyes were gazing upward, same as Graton's, in the direction of the being. Both had the same sense of frozen wonder and awe at this larger-than-life "Creator."

Asha and I stared at one another, both in shock. She was the only one who knew what I was feeling in that moment. I wanted to tell her I was sorry about her father, sorry about everything that was happening, but nothing came out.

Somehow, I think she knew what I wanted to say but couldn't.

She gently grabbed me and wrapped her arms around me. I hadn't been hugged in years, and so sincerely, and with such sadness.

From the corner of my eye, I could again see the being watching us with a strange sense of curiosity.

As Asha and I separated, it bent down to take a closer look, and I found myself face to face with the massive being. It squinted its eyes, as if it were trying to read me, see into me, into my soul.

Suddenly, a strange feeling overcame me.

"We should go … now," I said. "It's going to release the water. All of it."

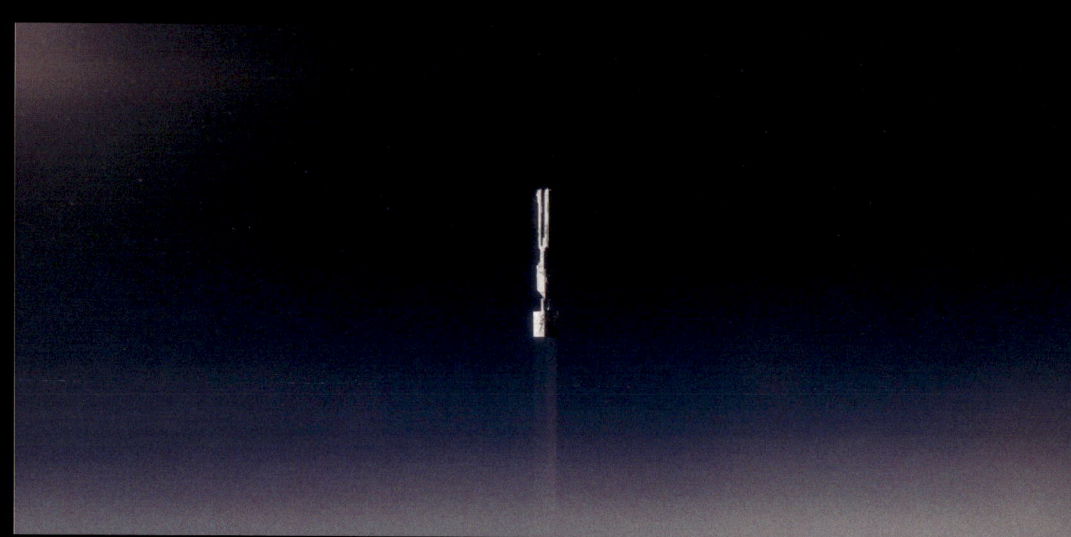

Unceremoniously, it rose and turned to what looked like a different control panel, and began what was clearly a different procedure. It again looked at us, then continued with its new work.

The large machinery's light went from blinking red to blue, and seemed to power down. The hum went silent.

Suddenly, small lights began blinking on the water tanks. We watched as they powered up row after row upward. That seemed to go on for infinity.

Whatever it saw in us, something changed its mind about what it was doing.

I quickly turned to Asha, and we both lifted the incubator and struggled to carry the small container that held what in nine months would be you.

We barely made it out as the huge ship began to pull the Citadel from the ground and upward.

The ground began to shake and crack under our feet. Centuries-old structures toppled and fell. The Oasis was crumbling before our eyes.

Then, zipping out from a dust cloud was the Widows Revenge.

The ship hovered above us and the captain lowered the boarding ramp. Several pirates leaned out and offered their hands.

Once the Citadel was free from the ground, it made a tremendous noise, the slits on the side opened and it began purging its water stores.

The pirates quickly lifted us into the ship. We had to weave our way through the hundreds of giant water geysers spewing from the building. As the ship banked and weaved, I looked at Asha, who clearly hadn't gotten her "space legs" yet either.

I grabbed her hand, and she held on tight.

As we flew away, the water below us pooled into what eventually would be known as Lake Serenity. It was a beautiful sight.

I breathed a sigh of relief as we plugged in the incubator.

We landed several miles away, with the rest of the terrified population. We all watched as the water spilled out. It seemed to take forever. Billions of gallons poured out into a nearby crater that had been its home a thousand years earlier.

They all watched as their homes, their old way of life, was destroyed by the very thing we'd all craved our entire lives - water. Now, we would rebuild and start new.

Once purged, the Citadel slowly lifted to the heavens and disappeared into the mothership. Below it a tremendous body of water. Only hints of what had been the Oasis remained. The water shimmered and reflected in the late afternoon sun. An odd calm seemed to replace the chaos of only moments earlier.

Things would change. A new society would form - a free society. It was a long road ahead, but the vast sea of blue made it an optimistic one.

In the long run, Sturges and his crew helped us form a trade route to other systems that allowed us new technologies and a chance at sustainability. New structures would form around the lake - farms, hospitals, homes.

I could then feel Asha's hand slip into mine. Soon, she would rally the people and create a new society, and, lucky for me and you, she would forever be an irreplaceable part of our lives.

But in that moment, I saw just a sad young woman mourning the loss of her father. She wiped the tears from her eyes. Although she had won her moral battle, she had to watch what for her was her infallible father slowly become, in her eyes, a zealous overlord.

In the end, I don't know if he was wrong about the Creators, or just misguided. I watched as the water poured forth, wondering if, ultimately, they did deem us worthy, just as he'd hoped.

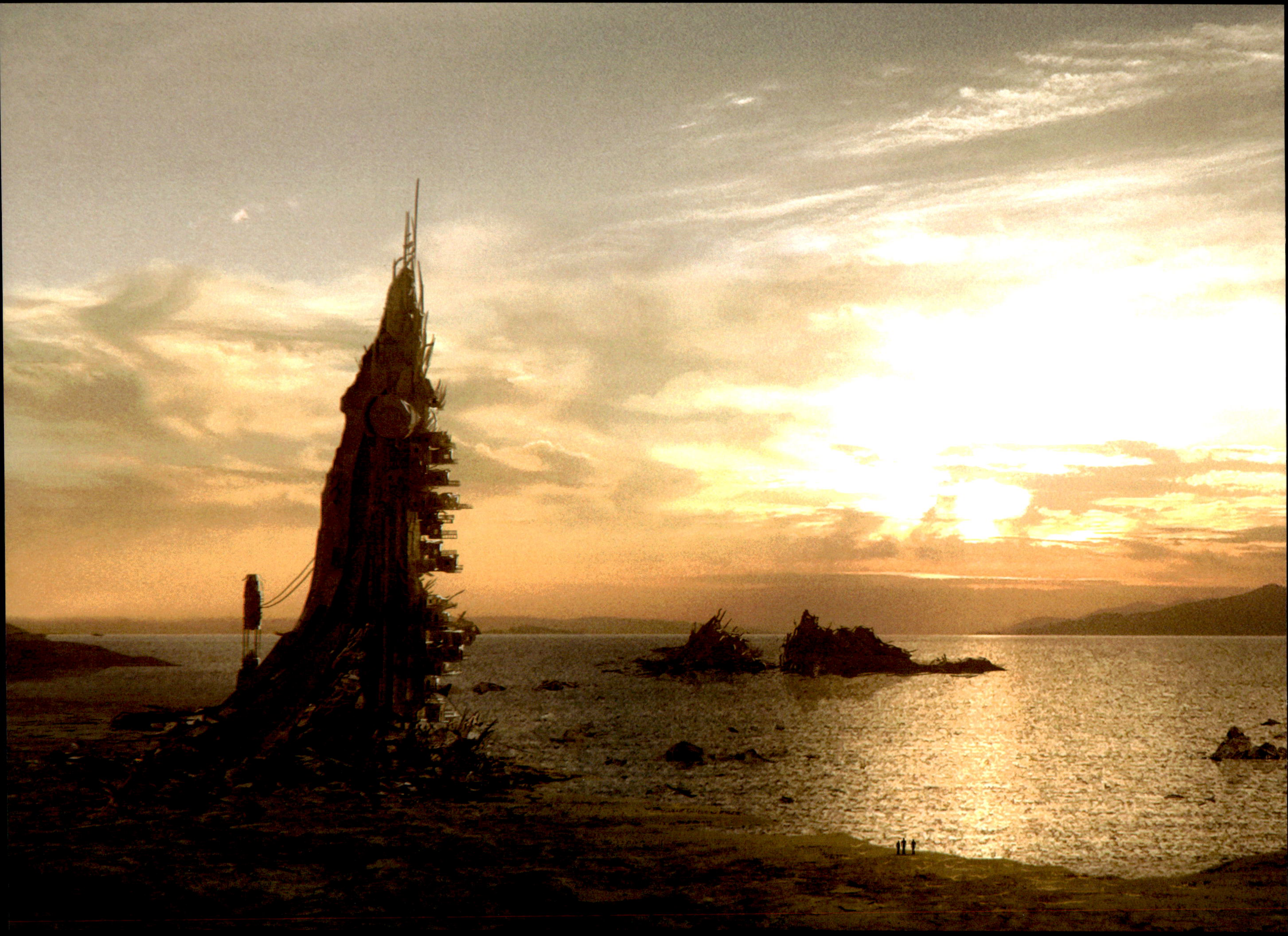

My thoughts quickly shifted to INC. His body rested within the structure. What I once saw as a glorified medical machine had become my conscience and, more importantly, my friend.

It's hard to accept the fact that I will never see INC again. But even harder to swallow is the fact that you will never know him - know his curiosity about the world, and his simple desire to learn.

Because he saw things the way we should all see things: with wonder and curiosity, but most of all, with hope.

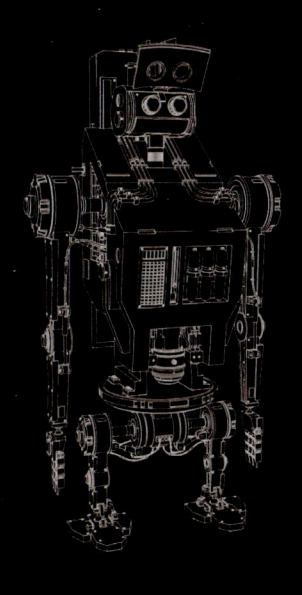

THE BOOK OF LANDIS

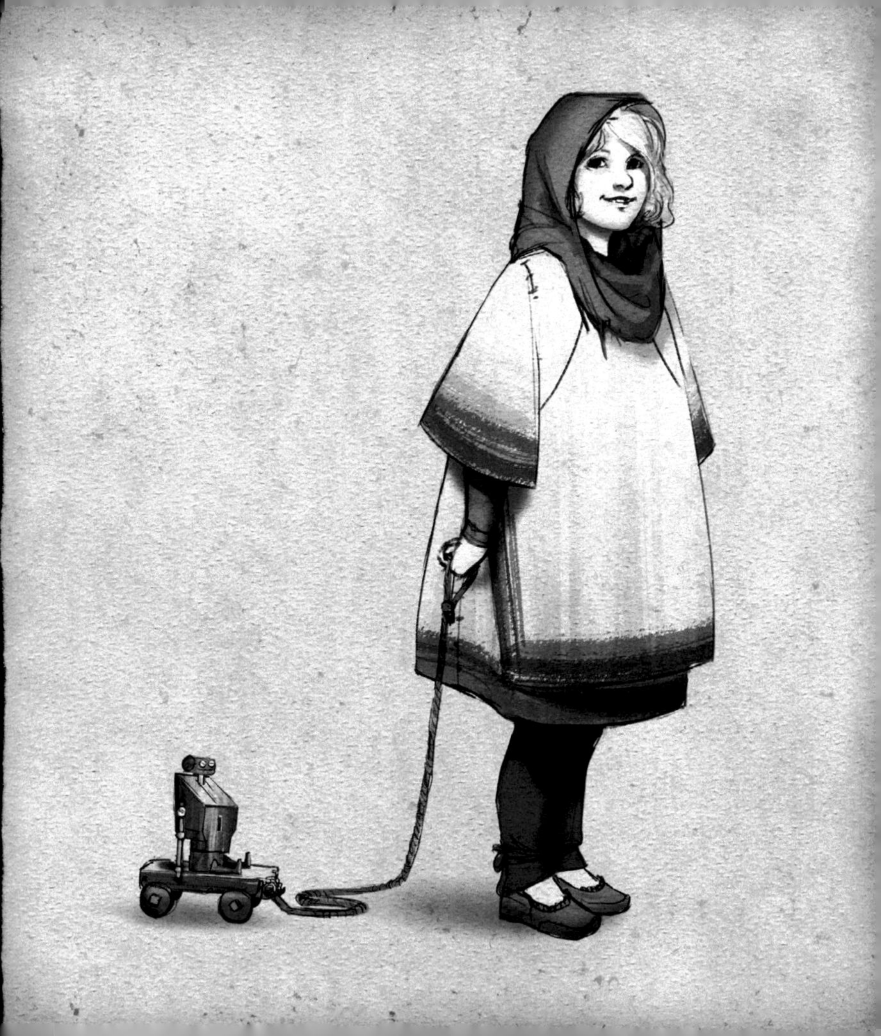

THE WORLD OF

△ INC △

While the Book of Landis is our best connection to the history of our people, there are other documents and images from the era that give us clues as to our people's story and the players that helped shape our current society. Where no imagery exists, we have done our best to recreate photos and diagrams to give you as clear a picture as possible, so that we may never forget the struggles that led to the rise of our current civilization.

—The Historian

The object on his back is a bag for carrying tools and supplies necessary for survival: water tap, food, medicine and hygiene supplies, and weapons.

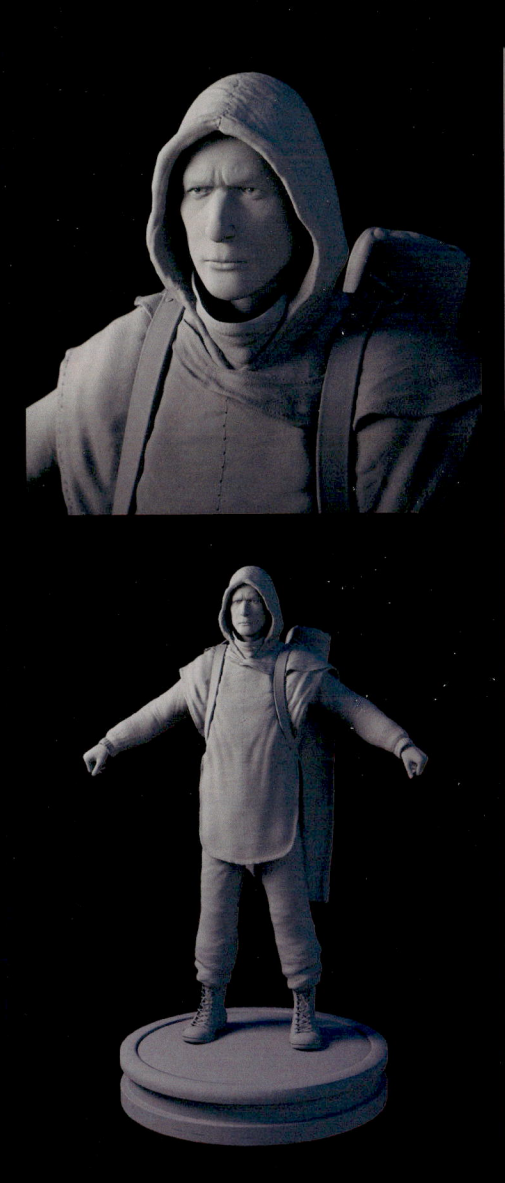

The primitive plant fiber and animal skin clothing he wears provided protection against our world's formerly harsh environment.

character

LANDIS

Landis, The Wanderer, father of the second age of our world, is shown here in an artist's rendering based on the few blurry, faded images of him which survive from his time, as well as descriptions of The Great Encounter (translated from the alien tongue, as few of our own records from that time survive).

His look of intense determination is common to all accounts, contemporary or otherwise. A man of few words, Landis was hardened by the desolation of his era, but not broken by it. All citizens can look to his example in times of despair.

THE STORY OF INC

character

INC

INC, Landis' companion of many years, his only friend during his time as a desert wanderer -- and the "mother" of his child.

INC started its life as a maintenance robot, a stalwart survivor from the time of the fallen fathers, its manufacturer and type number having been long forgotten even in the days of Landis.

INC's design featured hyper-zoom eyes with flip-up debris protection covers, heavy-lift arms, scoop-type hands, tri-stabilized feet and independent-drive hydraulic legs. Its systems were hardened and shielded for harsh environment operations, which is what allowed this robot to survive for so long.

INC may seem primitive by our standards, but during Landis' time this robot was beyond state-of-the-art. The device it carries is a pulse welder, not intended as a weapon but able to be used as one in a pinch.

THE WORLD OF INC

INC's Cryogenic Canister

124 THE STORY OF INC

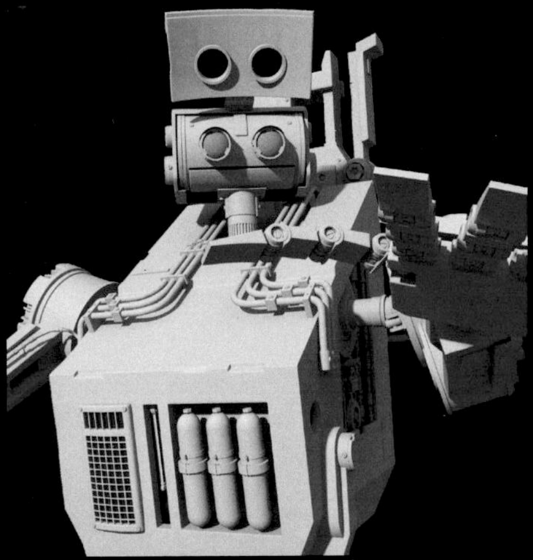
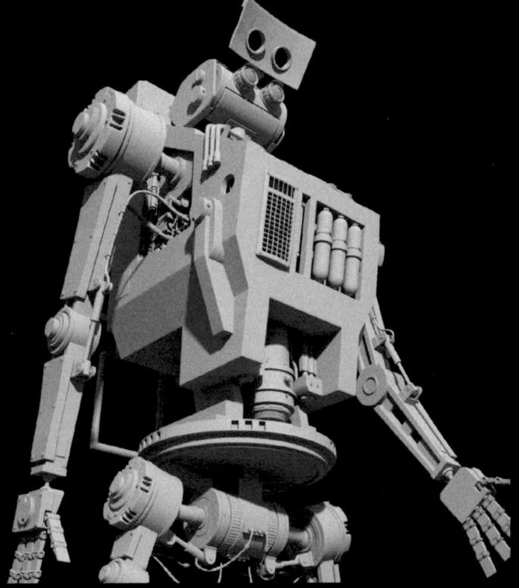
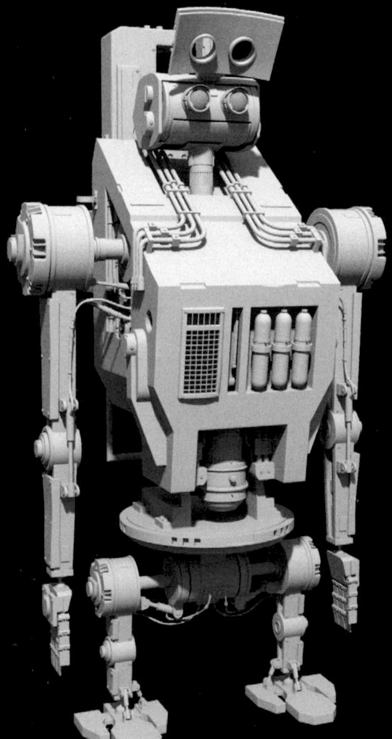
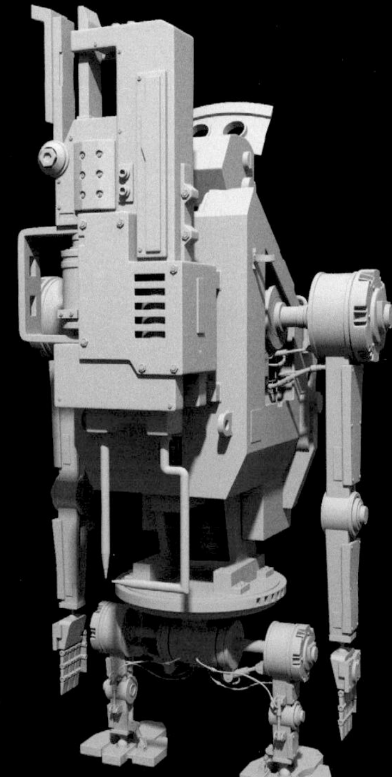
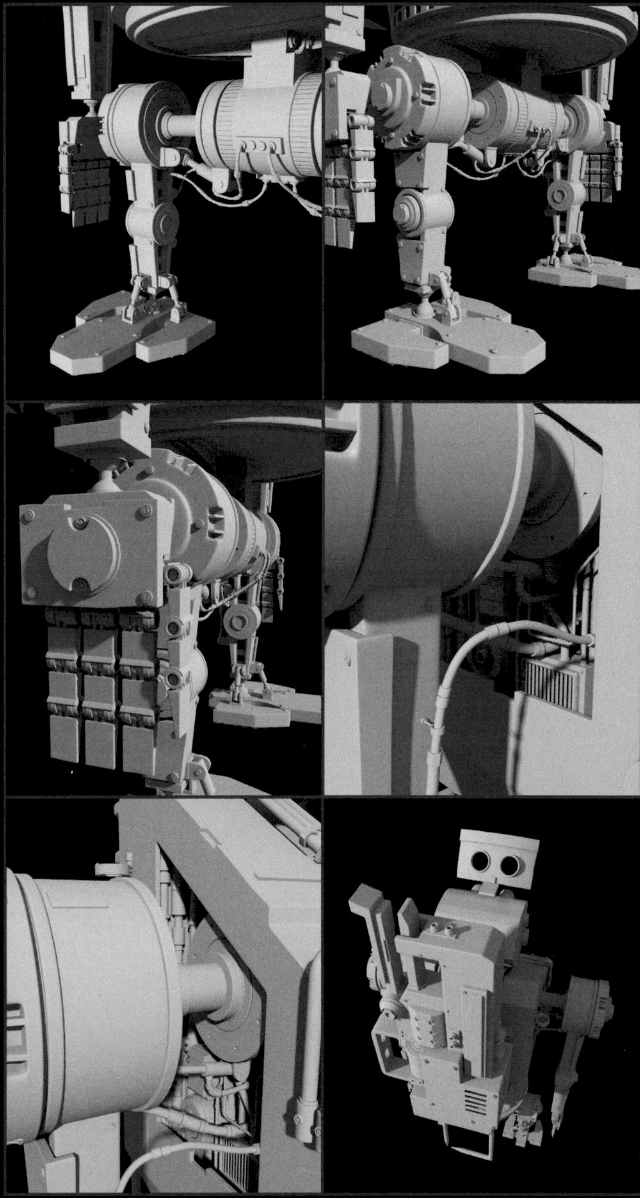

126   THE STORY OF INC

character

ASHA

Asha was born within the walls of Oasis, and grew up wondering why the bounty of the Oasis was not shared with the Wanderers who lived outside the walls. Empathetic, yet tough, Asha frequently helped newcomers adjust to the rules and regulations of The Oasis despite not agreeing with all the rules herself. Owing to her respect for their tenacity and devotion, she formed a special bond with Landis and his "pregnant" robot INC.

Because of her role in helping bring about both the downfall of the old Oasis leadership and in making contact with the aliens, Asha became a leader of her people during the rebuilding period immediately following the floods.

environment

THE DESERT

Despite years of travel by nomads and scouts alike, no one ever found an end to the desert region on our planet, which led many to suspect the entire planet was bone dry. So when it was revealed that the water on the planet had been harvested over centuries by hundreds of citadels placed on the surface by an ancient alien race, the pieces of the puzzle snapped together, and all of the geological questions asked over the centuries by our greatest minds were answered in one perfect moment of clarity.

The only break in the sand and rock that made up the desert region were strange giant plant life, that hinted of a time where water may have covered the entire planet. Most of this plant life was now fully fossilized, dried out husks of their theorized former glory. A few plants still contained miniscule reserves of water, and could be tapped by the particularly inventive nomad. But for the most part such structures were avoided lest they collapse on top of you if disturbed.

THE WORLD OF INC 129

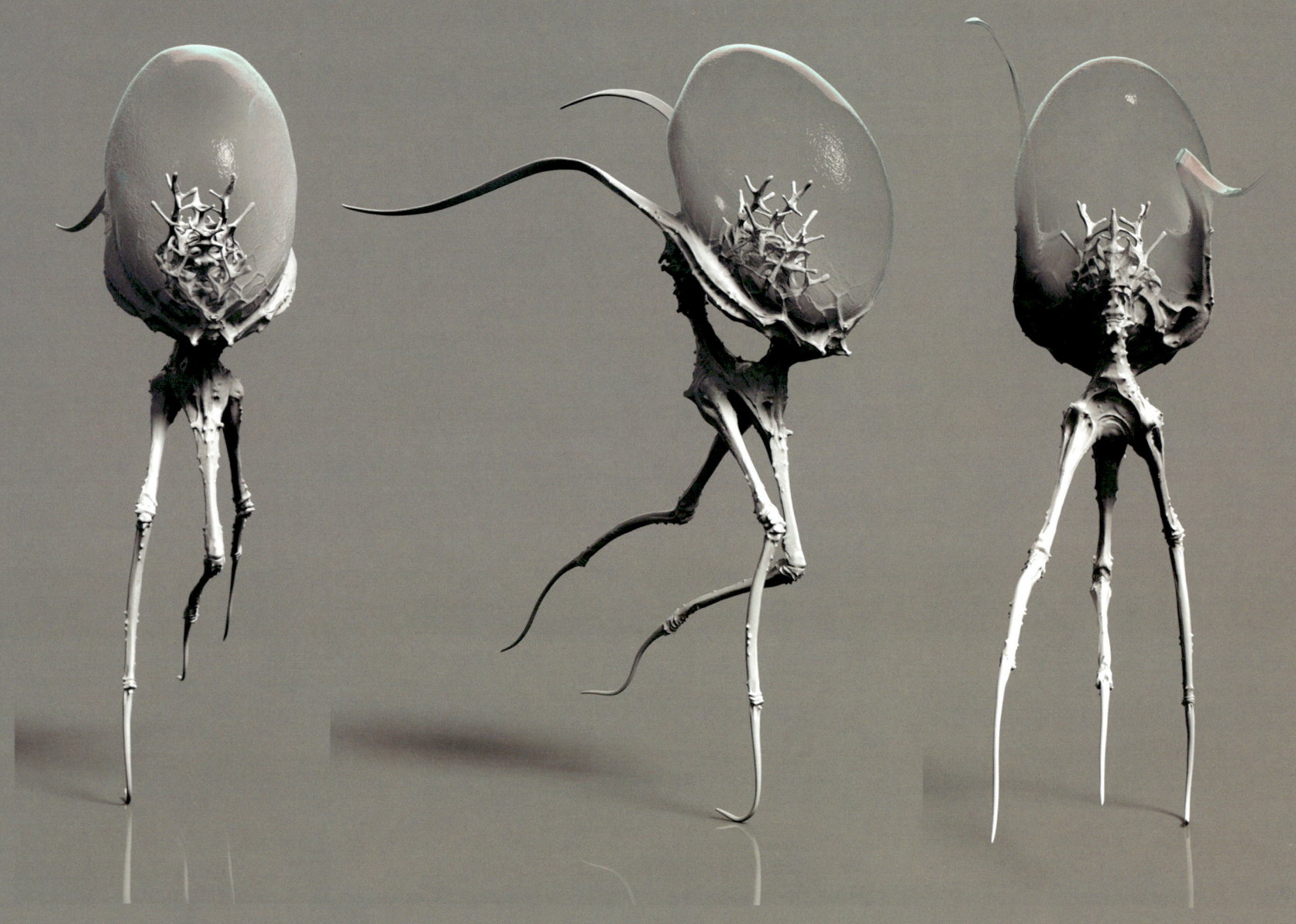

Many strange creatures roamed the desert, many of which could be deadly to man. Mutations introduced through interactions with alien species introduced into their environment during the fallen fathers' migration conflict with adaptation to their harsh environment resulted in numerous bizarre forms.

The Corallum is a night creature that prowls the desert when the temperature has gone down. They mimic the planets former underwater ecosystem in order to remain hidden, lure animals near, and then they strike with poison on their legs.

INC. | CORALLUM | DQWEK 2014

THE WORLD OF INC

INC. | STILTWALKER | DQWEK 2014

The Stiltwalker uses its long legs to keep its head above sandstorm dust while it travels in search of food and water. Its flat profile is also an adaptation to this environment, allowing it to cut through high winds like a blade. When it finds a water source, it uses its long tentacle like tongues to drink its fill. The long spikes on its rear portion make an effective defense against predators.

THE WORLD OF INC   133

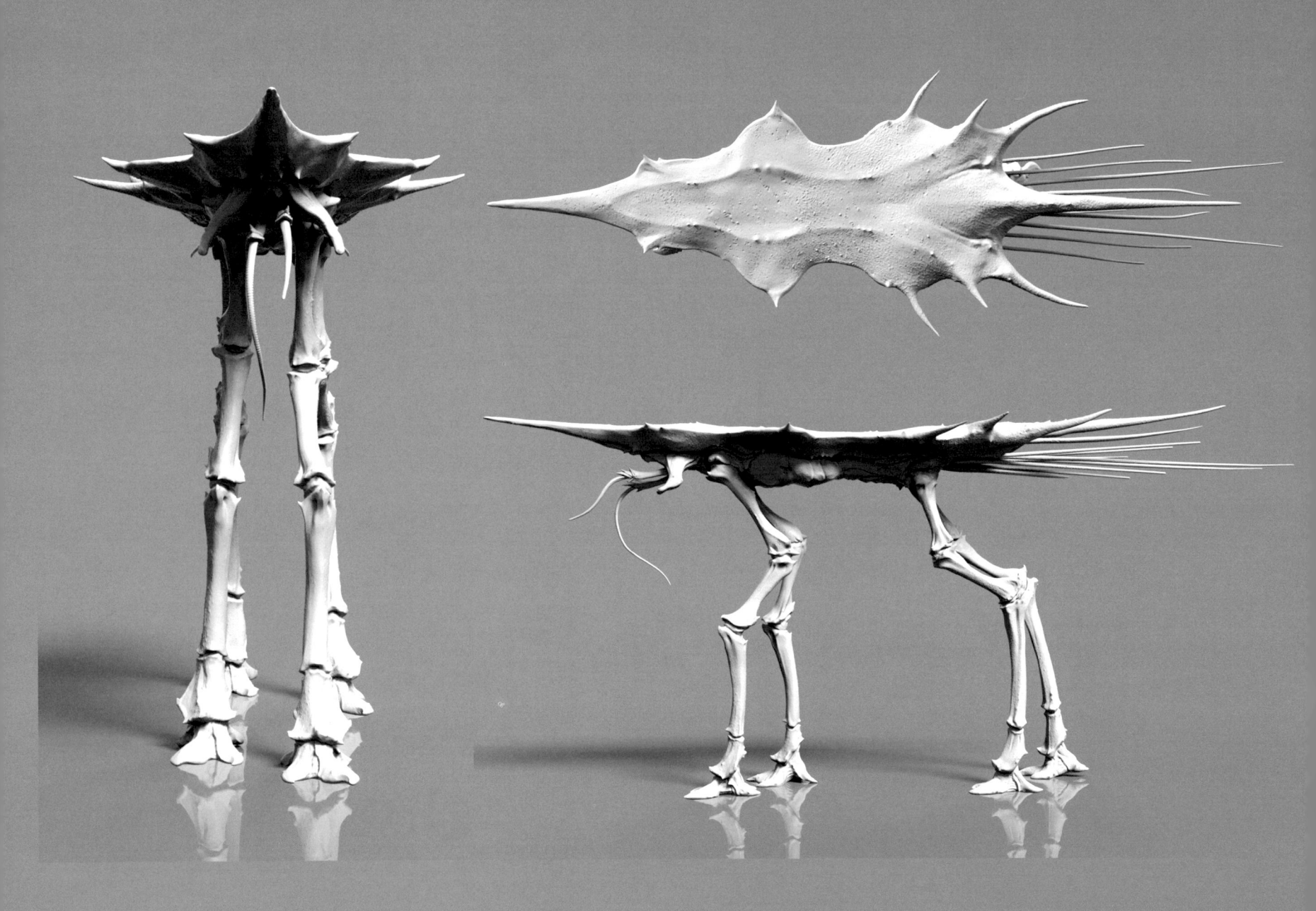

environment

THE OASIS

Built around the giant three-sided "Citadel" that contained the only known water source in the vast wasteland, other than the trickle obtained from the deep wells, The Oasis was designed to protect its inhabitants from outsiders and keep the water flowing to its residents. Vast walls with few, heavily guarded gates kept the nomads from entering The Oasis unbidden. Three towers inside the walls, one near each corner of the citadel, allowed the elders and guards to see any approaching nomad caravan no matter what the direction of approach.

Immediately within the walls were acres and acres of farmland, enough to grow all the food the inhabitants of the walled city needed to survive. Reinforced aqueducts piped water into the farmlands, with guards posted at each spigot to enforce the city's strict water regulations. The city core of merchants, workshops and residences formed a tight ring around The Citadel. Except for the farmers everyone in The Oasis lived and worked within a couple miles of The Citadel, with the tower guards keeping an eye on them as much as scouting for any approaching nomads. Rules were strict, punishment swift, and a rift between the elites and plebeians had grown such that by the time Landis and INC arrived many within the walls were as ready for change as those living in the wastelands.

THE WORLD OF INC 135

THE STORY OF INC

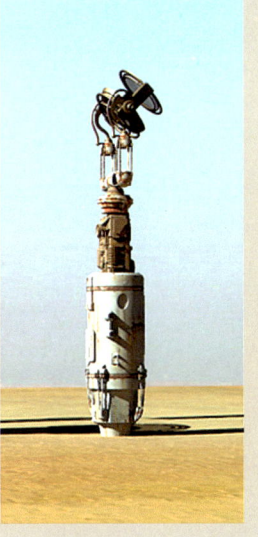

All water in the Oasis came from The Citadel, mostly that which leeched onto the skin of the monolith and ran down into the ground.

Since collecting extra water directly from the citadel was impractical due to the guardians other methods for collecting water were necessary to increase the water supply. This was an initial attempt involved using giant lenses. While the device was capable of vaporizing water pooling on the skin of the citadel, it did so in insufficient quantities to cause rain.

An early attempt at flight by the people of the oasis.

Sadly, the vehicle was never able to rise much more than a few feet off the ground, killing the settler's hopes for manned air travel.

The technology found other uses though, similar vehicles were routinely used to transport heavy supplies to different locations around the settlement, and to aid in the construction process of the main 3 towers.

THE WORLD OF INC

A) Citadel
B) Towers
C) Wall
D) Gates
E) Farmland

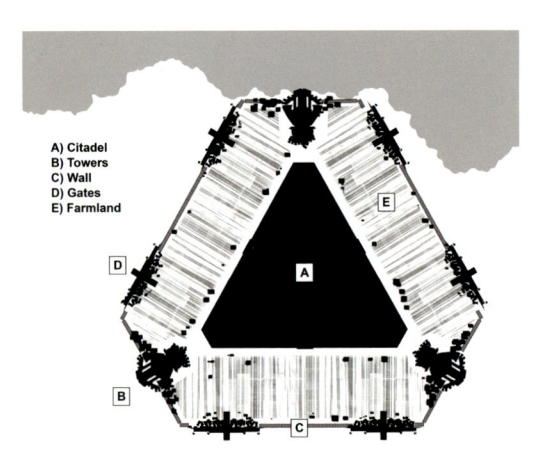

The ancients' most fruitful solution to their water collection problem involved employing creatures known as Lumadoptera, which had evolved seventeen stomachs to store up to a year's supply of water to keep them alive during their desert wandering. These winged creatures were trained to fly to the citadel, collect vast amounts of water in their stomachs, and then land atop one of the three Oasis towers and unload their water payload. Since water was plentiful at the Citadel the creatures could collect plenty to spare. For their part of this mutually beneficial relationship the Citadel Monks of Oasis fed and groomed the beasts, and kept them safe from predators.

THE STORY OF INC

THE WORLD OF INC

The water ran down the towers to the settlement below, energy being generated as gravity pulled the water through turbines in the towers.

Then the water would make its way into a complex aqueduct system and used for drinking, farming irrigation, and even bathing -- an incredible luxury to a desert wanderer, whose grooming consisted mainly of sand-scrubs. Only the Monks were permitted to operate the water supply system, leading to contention with not just the desert wanderers who were forbidden entry until a citizen died, but even with the citizenry themselves. Fortunately, our republic has learned the lessons of the ancients and no longer separates our citizens by caste.

THE WORLD OF INC   141

character

THE PIRATES

Pirates aboard "Widows Revenge" came to our world specifically to scavenge parts and technology that they could sell or use.

Destroying what many in Oasis considered Gods and robbing "the corpses of the God" led to violence between adherents of the old ways of Oasis, those wishing to cast-off those ways, and the Pirates themselves. It is not an exaggeration to say that the Pirates' arrival was the catalyst for the end of the first civilization.

THE WORLD OF INC   143

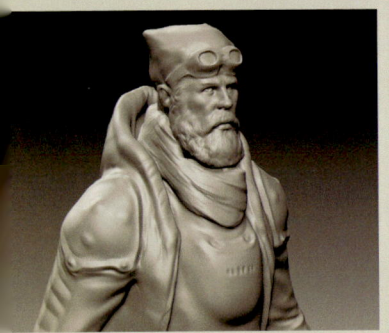

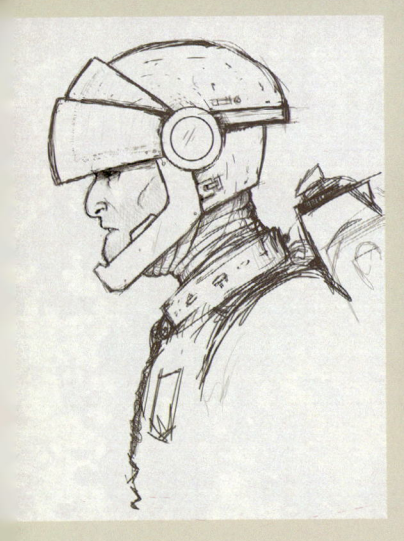

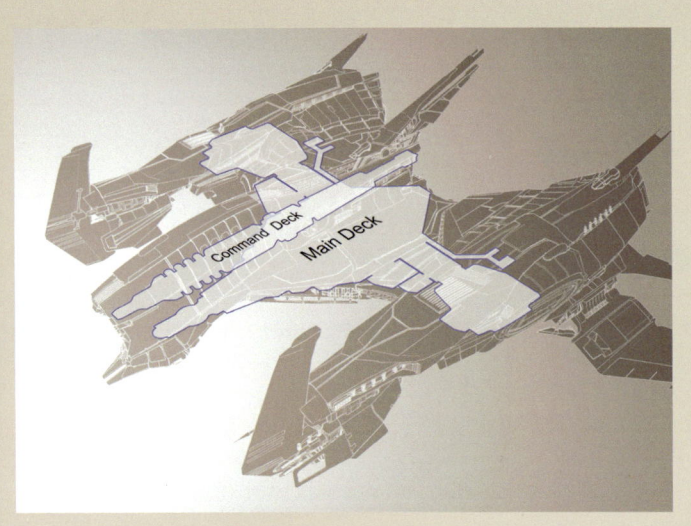

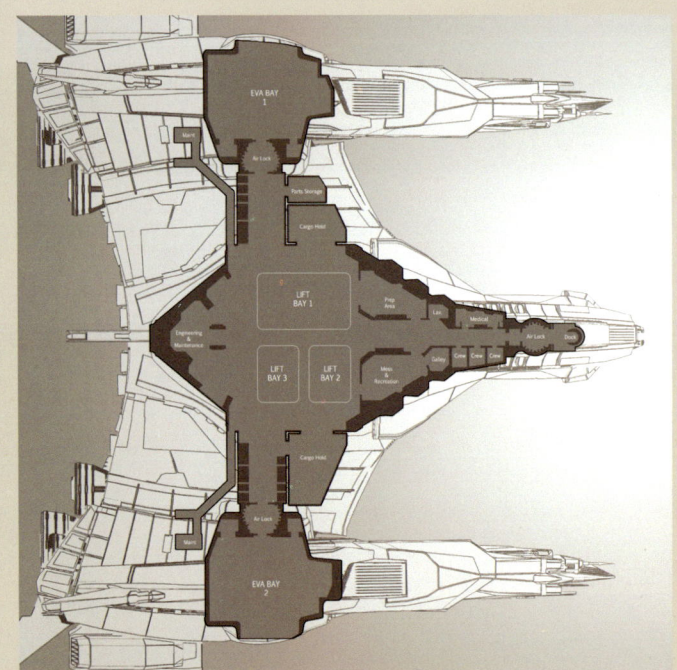

Schematics of the Widow's Revenge

144   THE STORY OF INC

THE WORLD OF INC   145

environment
THE CITADEL

Seeded onto a water-rich planet from the alien mothership by specialized ferry-dropper craft, the objects we came to call The Citadels would embed themselves several meters deep into the solid firmament beneath a planet's oceans and lakes. While pumps drew above-ground water into special ports on all sides of the harvesters, taplines were blasted down into the earth below to harvest the water table.

To accelerate the already lengthy process of collecting and processing that much water, explosives were ejected from the top of any harvester once it was above water, vaporizing nearby reservoirs and allowing steam to be drawn in through the intakes that were no longer in position to ingest water directly.

Thousands of harvesters were dropped on any given planet, but given our small population at the time and the great geographical distances between any given harvesters (across harsh, nearly impassable deserts) the only one known to our history is the one known simply as The Citadel of The Oasis.

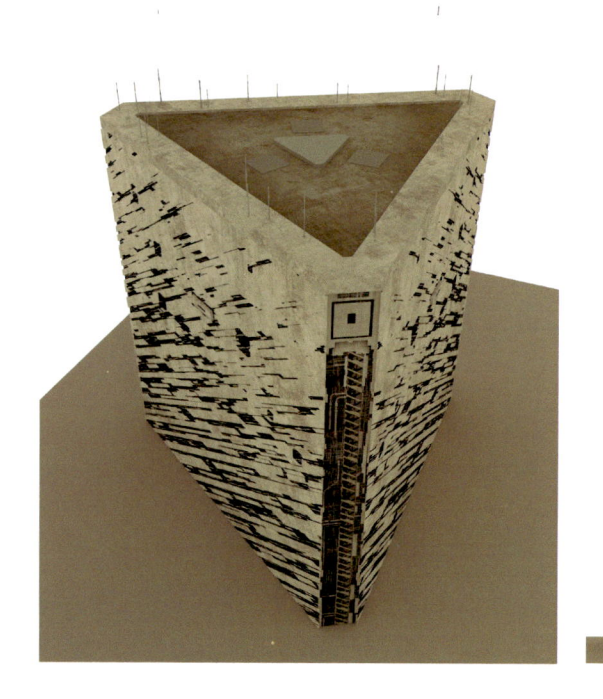

THE STORY OF INC

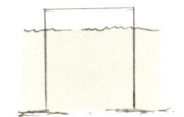

The Citadel is approx 0.5 miles or 2600ft (800m) wide and tall.

Place Citadel In Water

Set Off Bomb To Vaporize Water

Suck In Vaporized Water

Water Follows Pipes Downward

Water Stored In Underground Tanks

Water Converted To Energy

THE WORLD OF INC   147

character

THE GUARDIANS

The Citadel was protected by three Guardians, massive compared to a human, which the ancients considered to be minor deities sent by the Great God to guard their water supply.

They were feared and worshiped by the Citadel Monks of The Oasis.

Each guardian was primarily hidden underground in the loose sand, the only visible part was their ever watching statue like heads floating a few feet above the ground. But when provoked to anger by someone attempting to tap the Citadel water supply, they could unfold into heavily armed defense systems featuring bladed and energy weapons and moved using repulsors that enabled the guardians to traverse towards an intruder across any terrain. To the ancients the normally philosophical nature of Gods was rendered real in metal and light.

THE WORLD OF INC   149

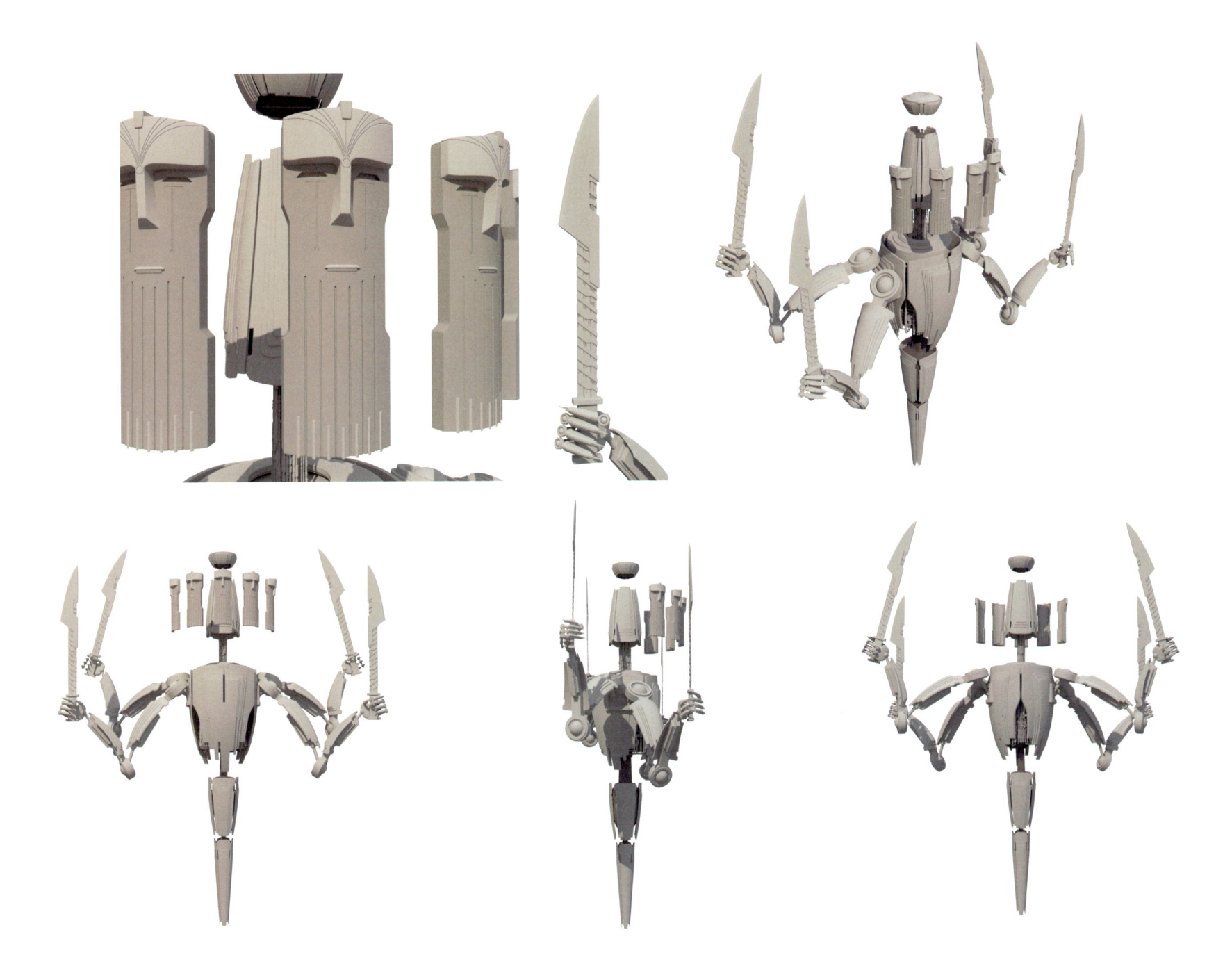

Despite the belief of the monks, the reality about the Guardians was far more mundane. They were in fact advanced security robots. Since The Citadel was a water harvesting device created by a very advanced alien civilization, these robots were intended to protect it from "vermin" that might arrive or evolve after the harvesting began (since the aliens' laws forbade harvesting water from inhabited planets).

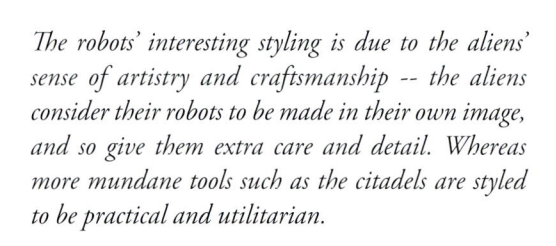

The robots' interesting styling is due to the aliens' sense of artistry and craftsmanship -- the aliens consider their robots to be made in their own image, and so give them extra care and detail. Whereas more mundane tools such as the citadels are styled to be practical and utilitarian.

THE WORLD OF INC   151

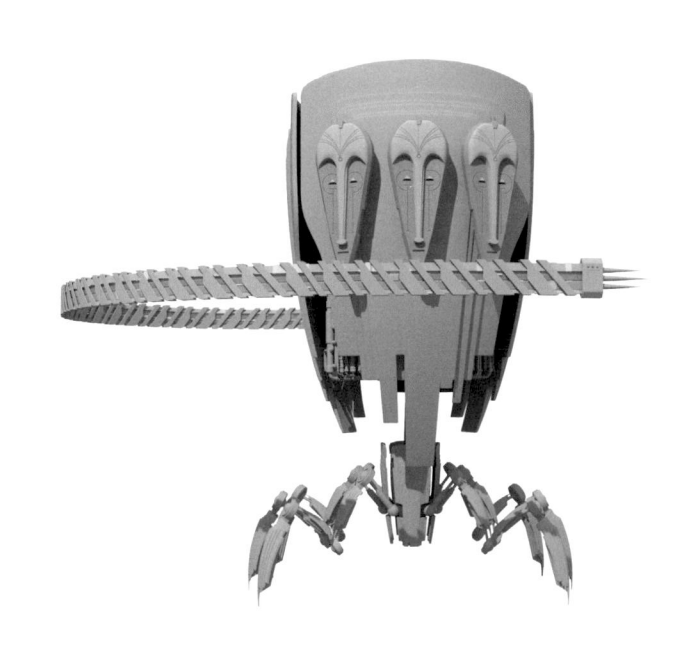

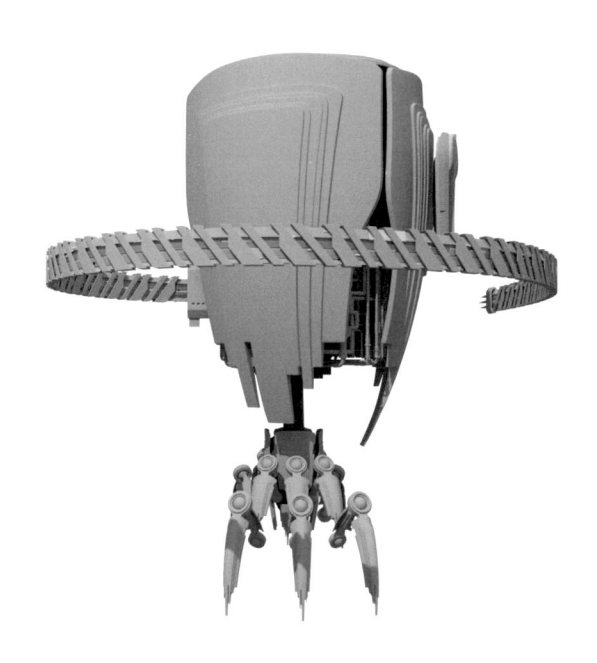

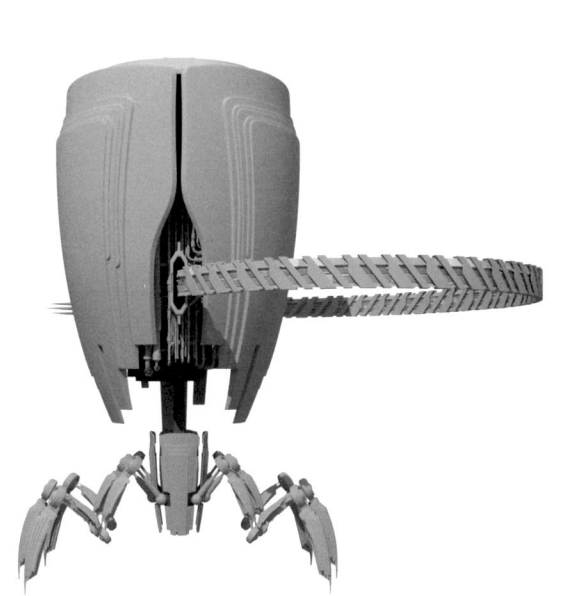

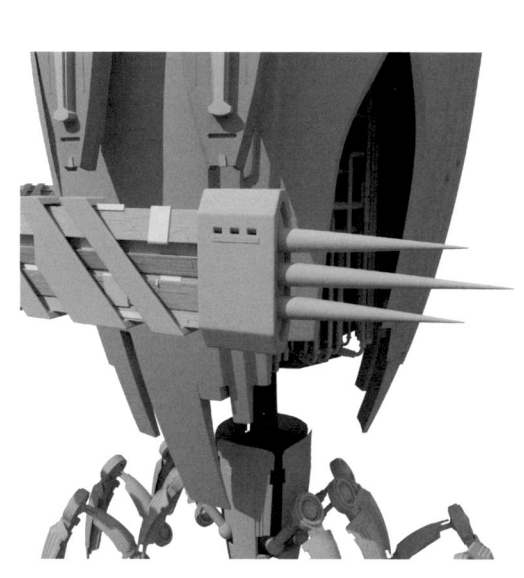

Three stages of Guardian robot were designed to deal with successively pernicious "vermin" (the aliens did not, until meeting Landis and INC, believe any lifeform as relatively small as ourselves was capable of sentience). The largest and final of the three added short-range conventional charge missiles to the mechanical-melee and energy weapons arsenals of its hierarchical predecessors.

Designed to ward off or eliminate primitive, pre-sentient lifeforms the Guardians were effective at keeping the lightly-armed and technologically underdeveloped people of The Oasis frightened and obedient.

Based on the events in our shared history the aliens realized the flaws in their understanding of intelligence and compassion, and have since redesigned their automated systems to detect and avoid harming less advanced, yet still sentient beings.

THE WORLD OF INC 153

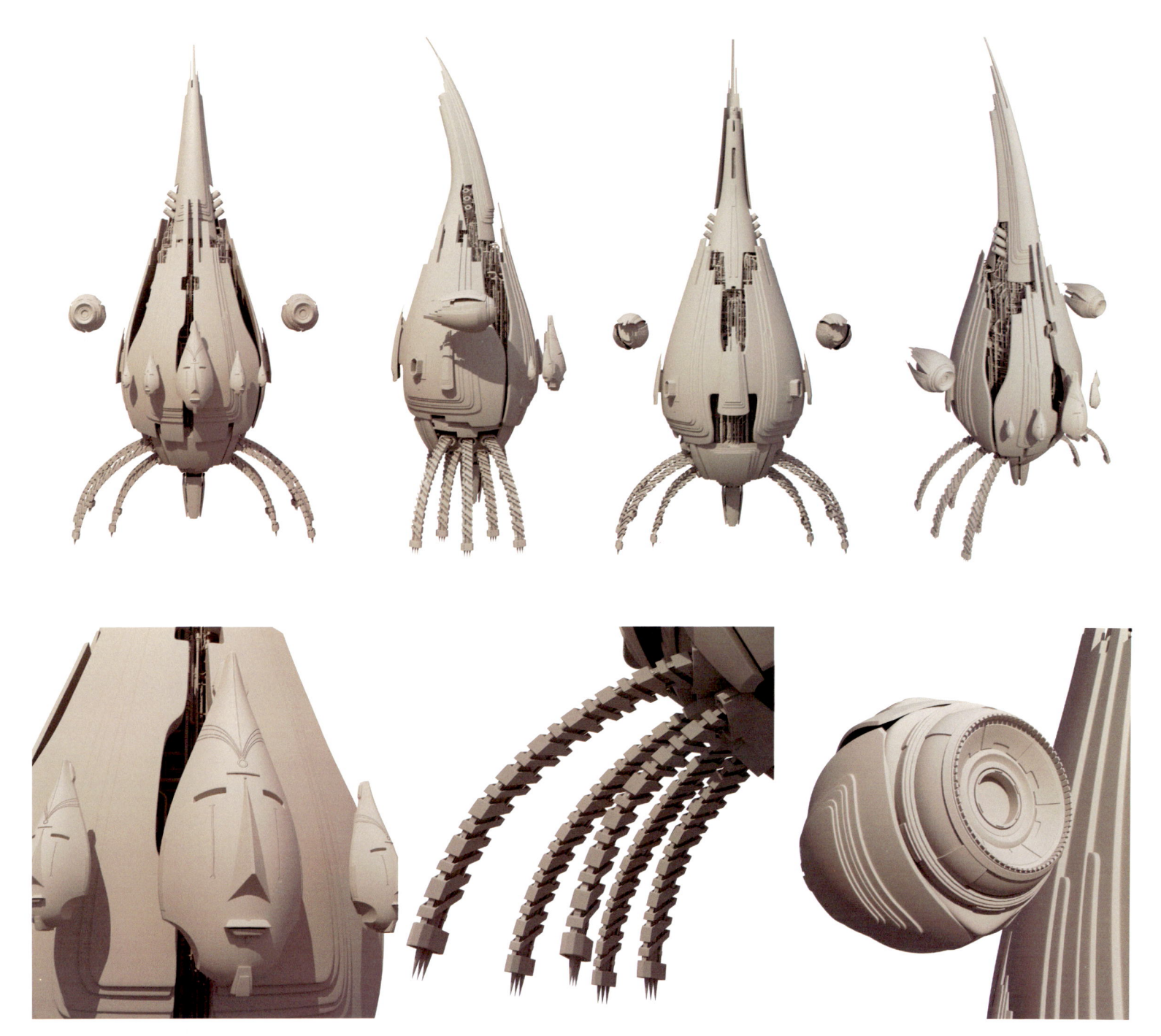

character

THE ALIEN

The Citadels were originally placed on our world, and others, by a race we simply know as "the aliens" as they refer to themselves in their own language by word that simply means "ourselves" (and which can not be transliterated into our language).

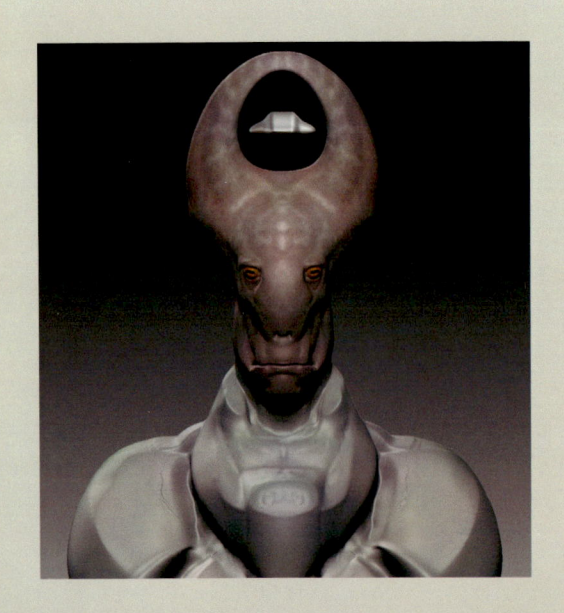

154   THE STORY OF INC

THE WORLD OF INC   155

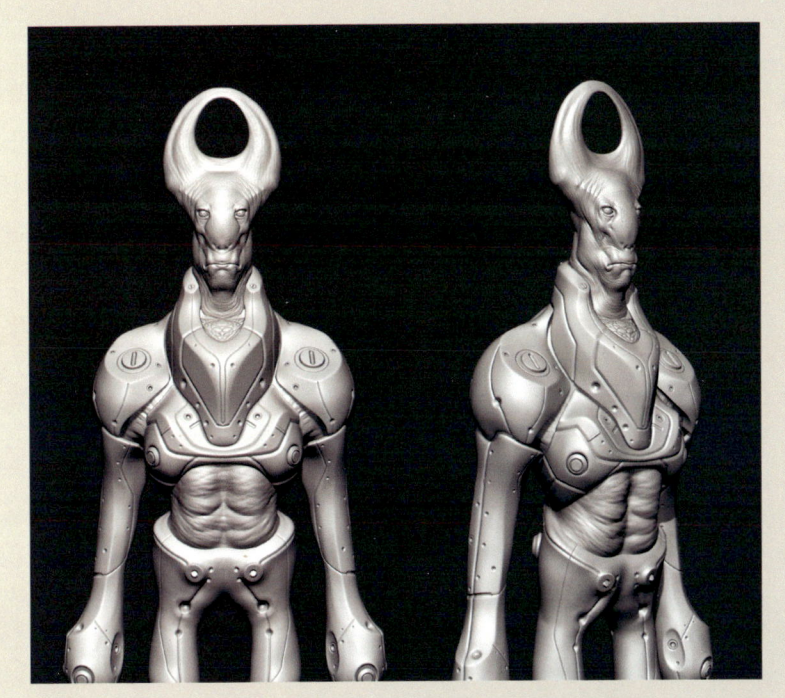

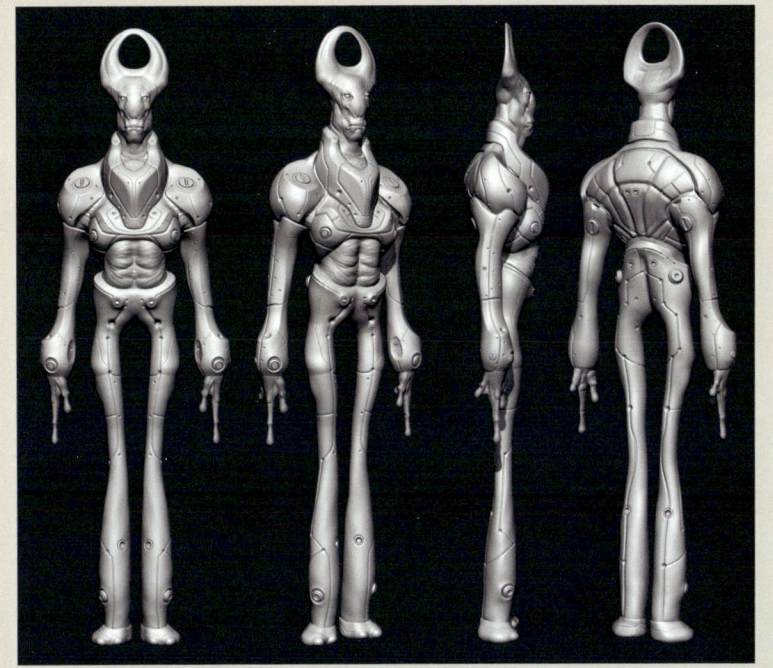

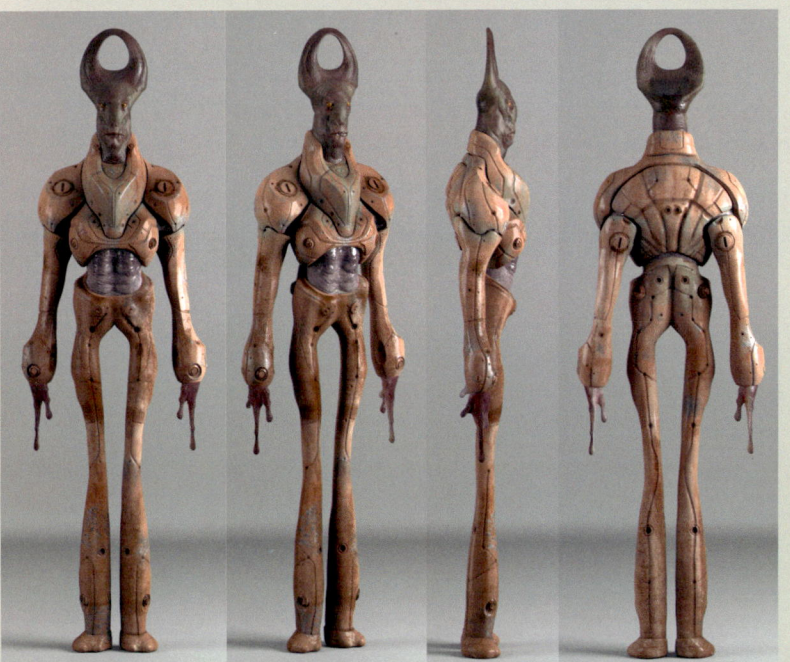

vehicle
THE MOTHERSHIP

Built to travel vast interstellar distances while carrying hundreds of the half-mile long citadels, and crewed by thousands, the harvester motherships are three hundred miles long and tens of miles wide.

These ships ferry empty harvesters to uninhabited, water-rich planets and then return to harvest them when the harvester beacons activate. Given the volumes of water and distances traveled involved, centuries often pass between dropping an empty harvester and returning to collect it -- a reasonable process for a race that lives for millennia.

Since the time of Landis the aliens have maintained peaceful relations with our people, but given our differences in technology, lifespan and origins we still only understand each other slightly.

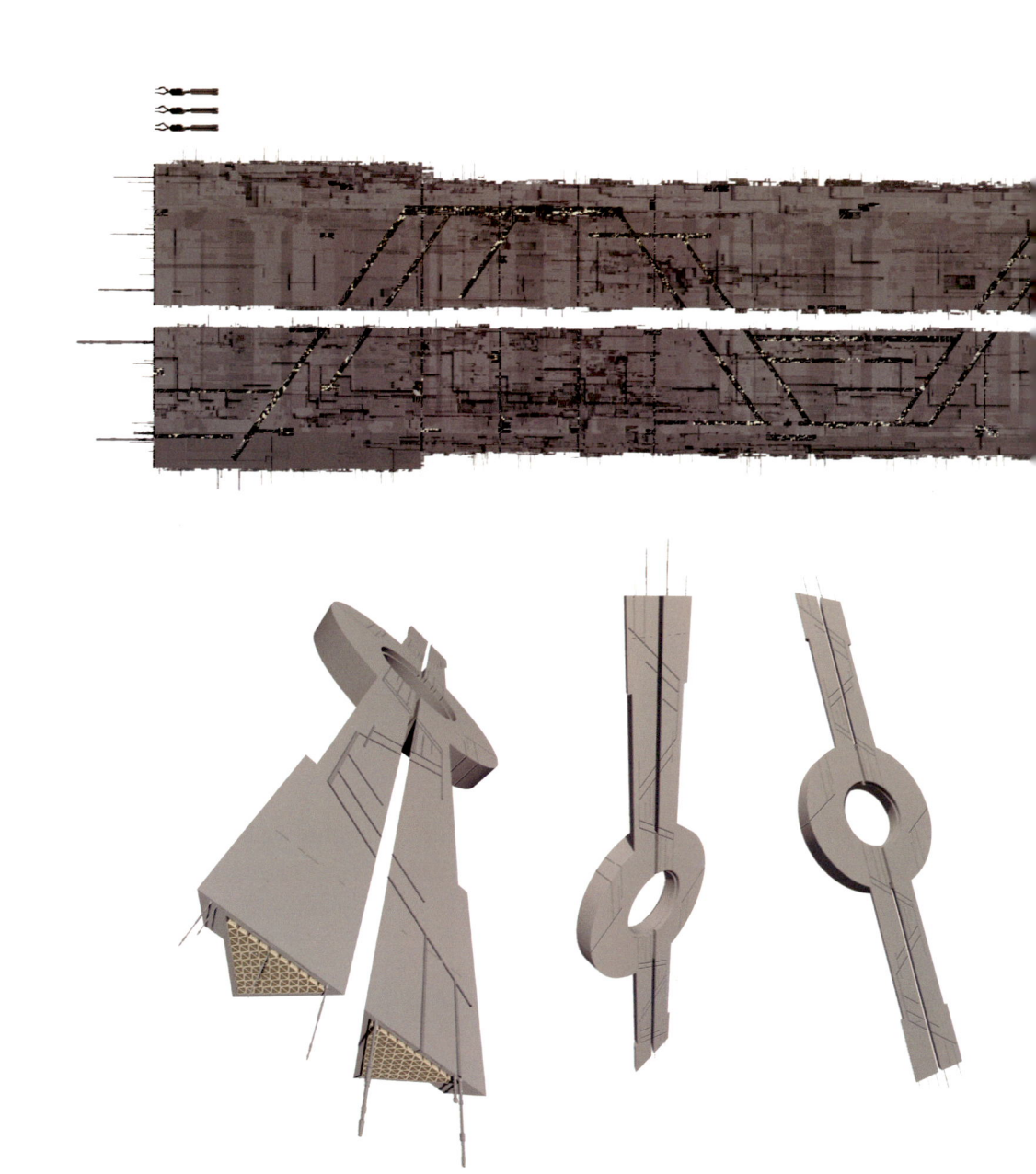

THE STORY OF INC

THE WORLD OF INC   157

THE MAKING OF

△ I N C △

To learn more about how the artwork was created for this book, please visit the following URL:

http://www.neilblevins.com/cg_education/inc/inc.htm

You will find written word tutorials, as well as almost 2 hours of detailed video tutorials showing the art making process.

How INC Came To Be...

For almost two decades, the vast majority of my personal artwork have been stand alone pieces. Each would have their own little narrative, but those narratives would always remained unconnected. I suppose it was partly because I was experimenting, partly because my ideas were varied, partly because the idea of a larger work seemed too daunting. But I'd keep making artwork, and when the public took a look they'd say "That's cool, so are these all part of some greater universe or story?" And I'd always have to say no. After being asked for the hundredth time, I started wondering if other people knew something I didn't.

As a kid, I loved the Original 80s transformers toys / TV show / comics, I watching Goldorak (Grendizer) fight a new giant monster robot each Saturday morning on French Canadian TV, and the original Star Wars trilogy of course, I was making snow walkers at age 4. Those universes were all so important to my development as a child and as an artist. And I continued to be inspired by new universes as I grew, until finally I realized it was time for me to make a larger work.

November 2013, I came up with several ideas, the one that seemed the most developed was the seed that sparked this finished work you see before you. But now came the daunting part. A 100+ page book all by myself? Humans? I'd much prefer to make robots and alien landscapes than humans. And then there was the mechanics of the story, while I've always enjoyed coming up with small ideas, I didn't have the writing chops to do the compelling story I wanted to go with the artwork.

That's where my buddy Bill Zahn came in, we'd worked together at Blur and Pixar, Bill's humans always had such character, and imagine that, he's also been focusing for quite some time writing film scripts. The match seemed perfect! He took my original idea and changed it around substantially into a much stronger idea, the ultimate goal of any collaboration. Then another friend Stephan Bugaj joined the team to help strengthen the story even further.

But I felt we needed more help, I wanted varied styles of artwork (not to mention we needed to create close to 500 pieces of art for the project).

So I called on a number of artist friends; Jeremy Cook was another ex-blur buddy who has since also worked at ILM, id Software, and now 343 Industries as an art director. His robot and military vehicle designs have always been kickass, so I was super excited when he agreed to join in. Chris Stoski laid down the foundation for the Oasis, Christina Davis filled in character sketches, Jeremy V, Gio, Dominic, Heidi, Nathan and Mohammad, all amazingly talented artists who helped flush out the world of Inc to keep it rich and diverse, and bringing amazing ideas to the table to enhance our original vision.

So here you have it. A book that may be a bit tough to classify. I like calling it an "Art Of Book for a Film that doesn't exist". Bill likes calling it our "Picture Book For Adults". Perhaps its really a "Modern Illustrated Novel". Whatever you want to call it, I hope you've enjoyed our fusion of Words, Imagery and Science Fiction.

This is just the beginning...

Neil Blevins

NEIL BLEVINS

Director /
Production Designer / Story

Neil Blevins started off painting and drawing traditionally, and then got into digital art while still living in his home country of Canada. After getting a BFA in Design Art, he moved to Los Angeles where he worked for Blur Studio. He now lives in San Francisco working as a Digital Artist for Pixar. In his spare time, he makes sci-fi 3d/2d hybrid artwork, author tools and writes art related lessons and tutorials for his website.

neilblevins.com

BILL ZAHN

Concept Art / Story /
Writer (Journal)

Bill Zahn was a kid obsessed with movies. At the age of nineteen, he packed his bags and with sixty bucks to his name, moved to Los Angeles to chase his dream. He quickly made his way into the world of live action creature and make-up effects, working on projects like Men in Black, Godzilla and the Budweiser Frogs. After successfully working ten years in LA, he made the transition to the digital world, working for studios such as ILM, Tippet Studios and, currently, Pixar Animation Studios. For the past six years, he has rekindled his passion for writing and has several projects in development.

billzahn.com

STEPHAN BUGAJ

Story / Writer (Historian)

Stephan Bugaj started screenwriting professionally at Pixar Animation Studios, having transitioned from a decade of working as a technical artist to co-creating two development projects. He subsequently left the studio to head-up all writing and directing for Telltale Games. He then headed to Los Angeles where he works as Creative Director for Hanson Robotics and as a film, games and virtual reality writer-director working with WakingUp Media, Visioneer Studios, Marza Animation Planet, Digital Quilt, Limitless VR and many others.

bugaj.com

JEREMY COOK

Concept Art

Jeremy Cook has been a digital artist for nearly 20 years. He has been in film, games and cinematics. Working with; Blur Studio, Industrial Light + Magic, id Software, and currently, 343 Industries.Creating models, matte paintings and concept art on projects including; Transformers 1, Star Wars EP3, Mission Impossible 3, Day After Tomorrow, Nuthin' But Mech, Halo, Doom as well as countless TV commercials, cinematics and magazine covers. As an Art Director at 343 Industries, he works with crazy, talented artists to ensure the games you play, look good. When not working, he loves spending time with his family and expanding his hoodie collection in the beautiful Pacific north west city of Kirkland.

2d2cg.blogspot.com

CHRIS STOSKI

Concept Art

Chris graduated from the School of Architecture at Washington State University in 1994, and soon transitioned to the film industry working at San Francisco's Matte World Digital as a Matte Artist. He then joined Industrial Light and Magic where he worked on Star Wars Ep 3 and Pirates Of The Caribbean 2, followed by a supervisory role for Pirates 3, Iron Man and Star Trek. Chris then joined IMD as a concept artist working with lead designer Doug Chiang on The Yellow Submarine and Robota. In 2011 Chris joined Atomic Fiction where he has done concept and art direction for Looper, Flight and Star Trek: Into Darkness. He continues to work in the entertainment industry as an art director and concept artist.

stoskidigital.com

CHRISTINA DAVIS

Concept Art

Christina Davis is a freelance Illustrator and Fine artist based in San Francisco, California. She studied classical realism at both Safehouse Atelier and Sadie Valeri Atelier, which built a strong traditional foundation that influences all of her work. Since beginning her entertainment art career in late 2011, she has contributed to several franchises including Star Wars, Transformers, and Lord of the Rings.

artchimera.carbonmade.com

JEREMY VICKERY

Concept Art

Jeremy started his art career as a chainsaw sculptor, but after too much sawdust up the nose decided that computers were better. He's worked as a Lighting Artist at Pixar, and as a freelance illustrator for clients such as Disney, Sony, LEGO, Ubisoft, and more. Bound by wanderlust he travels the planet in search of magic and art inspiration.

http://jermilex.blogspot.com/

DOMINIC QWEK

Concept Art

Dominic Qwek is a creature and character artist. He loves making monsters, aliens and creepy beings of all manner. He currently works at Blizzard Entertainment as a senior cinematic artist where he gets to do more amazing art. Apart from spending most of his free time on art, Dominic enjoys petting his cats and long strolls on the beach with his wife.

dominicqwek.com

HEIDI TAILLEFER

Concept Art

Heidi Taillefer is a fine artist living and working in Montreal, Quebec. She spent 10 years as a professional illustrator before dedicating herself full time to fine art, producing work that is a biomechanical hybridization often exploring classical themes addressing the human condition. Taillefer's work is exhibited across North America in gallery and museum venues.

heiditaillefer.com

GIO NAKPIL

Concept Art

As a child growing up in Manila, Giovanni Nakpil was greatly influenced by the magic of sci-fi and horror films. After studying Computer Graphics in Toronto, his multidisciplinary career led him to Maryland, Texas, California, and Washington. As a digital model supervisor for Industrial Light and Magic, Giovanni worked on principal creatures for "Star Trek" and "The Avengers," amongst other notable Hollywood films. He then switched gears by designing and building video game assets for Valve Corporation. Giovanni currently works at Oculus, where he is pushing himself even further, helping to define the look of VR.

gionakpil.com

MOHAMMAD MODARRES

Concept Art

Mohammad Modarres was born in Isfahan, Iran. In early childhood he discovered his strong passion toward the arts, especially drawing. Mohammad graduated in craft and design in 2006 and moved to Tehran where, among other roles, he was involved with Garshasp games as their senior character artist. After moving to San Francisco CA 2012, he has been an active part of Pixologic's Zbrush beta testing team and working as a freelance digital sculptor with McFarlane Toys on projects like Assassin Creed, the Walking Dead, and Halo, as well as publishing articles in 3dartist magazine and video tutorials for Uartsy. He recently joined Anatomytools team on an unannounced project.

3mmart.com

NATHAN FARISS

Model Maker

Nathan Fariss wants to live in a world where the only shows on television are about cars and how things are made. As a 3d Technical Artist, he's worked for over 15 years in freelance illustration, film and commercial visual effects and now animated features. His illustration clients include Popular Mechanics and Fortune Magazines and his film credits include Inside Out, Toy Story 3, The Host and Sin City. When he's not pushing pixels around a dimly-lit office, he'll be hunched over his model desk, trying to create the perfect rust spot on a six inch tall robot.

hello-napalm.com

ARTIST CREDITS

pg7-16: Neil
pg18: Bill
pg21: Neil
pg22-23: Neil-Bill
pg24(L): Neil
pg24(R): Jeremy V
pg25: Neil
pg26(L): Neil-Bill
pg26(R): Jemery V
pg27: Neil
pg28: Bill
pg29: Neil
pg30: Neil-Bill-ChrisS
pg32: ChrisS
pg34: Neil
pg35: ChrisS
pg36-38: Neil-Bill
pg39: Neil
pg40: Bill

pg42-44: Neil
pg46: Neil-Bill
pg47: Neil
pg49: Heidi
pg50: Neil
pg52: JeremyC
pg54: Neil
pg55-56: JeremyC
pg58: Neil-Bill-Christina
pg60: Mohammad-Neil-Bill
pg 61-62: Neil
pg 64: Neil-Bill
pg 65-76: Neil
pg79: Neil-Bill
pg 80-84: Neil
pg 86-89: JeremyC
pg90: Neil-ChrisS
pg92(UL): Neil
pg92(LL): Neil-Bill

pg92(R): Neil
pg94-96: Neil
pg97: Neil-Bill
pg98-99: Neil
pg100-101: Neil-Bill
pg102: JeremyC
pg103: Neil
pg104: Neil-Bill
pg107: Neil-Mohammad
pg108: Neil-Mohammad-Bill
pg110-113: Neil
pg114: Neil-ChrisS
pg117: Christina
pg:120-121: Bill
pg122:125: Neil
pg126-127: Christina
pg128-129: Neil
pg130-133: Dominic
pg134(T): Neil

pg134(M-B): Christina
pg135-136: Christina
pg137: ChrisS
pg138(TL): Neil
pg138-141: ChrisS
pg142-143: JeremyC
pg144(TL): Gio
pg144(BL): Bill
pg144(M): Mohammad
pg144(R): JeremyC
pg145: JeremyC
pg146-153: Neil
pg154(L): Gio
pg154(R): Mohammad
pg155: Mohammad
pg156-157: Neil
pg161: Neil

The Artists and writers wish to thank our wives and husbands, our girlfriends and boyfriends, our parents and children, and all our close friends who've given us the support and inspiration to bring this project to life.

For more info on the World of Inc, visit
http://thestoryofinc.blogspot.com/
http://www.facebook.com/thestoryofinc
http://thestoryofinc.tumblr.com/